---

# ONCALL
## Escorting in Atlanta

---

TO: Zakiyyah

I hope your world travels
brings you stories to write about

Ceasar Mason

8/17/17

# ONCALL

## Escorting in Atlanta

CEASAR MASON

770EMPIRE PUBLISHING · ATLANTA, GEORGIA

OnCall
By Ceasar Mason

770Empire Publishing
P.O. Box 132, Conley, GA 30288
www.ceasarmason.com
ceasarmason@gmail.com

ISBN-13: 978-0-9838166-0-7
ISBN-10: 0983816603
Library of Congress Control Number: 2011914093

Editing Services: DCselfpublishingsupport@gmail.com
Book Layout/Design: DCselfpublishingsupport@gmail.com
Cover Design: LaMont Carson,
Basementsoul.com, djx@basementsoul.com
Cover Photography: Gabriel Hart, GabrielHart.com
Cover Model: Adrienne Robins

First Edition
10  9  8  7  6  5  4  3  2  1

PRINTED IN THE UNITED STATES OF AMERICA

# DEDICATED TO

**Lilise Mason**, *daddy's little princess.*

If I've questioned anyone's love, I have no doubt about the love you have for your daddy. Thank you for all the hugs and kisses over the past years and those years to come. I pray that you never use your body to justify an ends to a means. As long as blood runs through my veins I'll always and forever be a provider for you.

To all the women in the sex trade looking for a way out!

# ACKNOWLEDGEMENTS

First and foremost I'd like to give all the glory to our Father. Thank You for Your Grace, Mercy and Wisdom. To my little princess, Lilise, to whom this book is dedicated to, we shared tears of joy and in your nine-year-old interpretation, you said, "I won't tell anyone daddy was crying." You understood that was our moment before I did. You and your brother Brian are my perpetual source of energy.

Carol Mason, mom you're still mothering after thirty some odd years. I love you and I'm extremely proud to call you my mother. Clibert Copeland, my father, you were really misunderstood and brilliant. R.I.P., much love, your son. Roger and Stephen, my older and younger brothers—thank you for always being there for me in one capacity or another. I'd also like to thank my brothers: (Alphabetical order) Andre "Ak" Kenan, Aubrey "Beets" Kenan, we all miss you bro', R.I.P. homie, Dehaven Irby, keep doing you homie, Dexter Ferary, Darren Ferary R.I.P. bro, Emory Jones, I'm glad you made it to this run, this is going to be a much better run, Gabriel Hart, Kenji Kenan, Keldon Quammie, Sean Pryor, and Young Jack Thriller. I must thank my sisters as well, Debbie Cadet, Jentura McArthur, Julia Hill your infectious smile and vast vocabulary, Tamika Byrd, Tisha Simon a.k.a. Mo'Brown for your listening ears, and Trina Swindell-Thompson thank you for your cheer and eternal optimism. Tanya Lewis for your encouraging words and corporate savvy, Lesah thanks for all your prayer and edification. Michelle Davis you were here from the conception of this book. I miss you dearly friend (July 1st). Smile! Krystal

Wright you are Love and my Angel, thanks for keeping my lights on. Uncle Michael Edwards, you're neither my father nor my mother's brother but you're indeed my uncle and much more. Thank you for being a man of compassion, character, and integrity. You have loved me unconditionally for over twenty years now.

To author and surrogate mother of hundreds of books, Karen E. Quinones Miller. You selflessly lend your experience to countless numbers of aspiring writers like myself. Thank you. To Jason Itzler, the best that ever did this. Allison Pickens my wing woman and homie. June Gilbert for your research and insight on the human trafficking summit. Thank you to DCselfpublishingsupport@gmail.com for your professional services.

# PREFACE

*O*ncall: Escorting in Atlanta, was inspired by my actual experience running an escort service in Atlanta for several years. In no way did I write this book to romanticize the industry like so many books and movies have done in the past. I wanted to take my reader on a call with one of these young ladies. I would like the world to see these women as more than dismissive objects that "made bad decisions." I want my reader to bear witness to the shame and indignity that these girls harbor within their spirits. The reader will get a front row seat to what lengths people will not only literally sell themselves but what they sell emotionally, spiritually and most importantly psychologically. I wrote this book from a fictitious standpoint to protect those who may not want to publicly share the darker periods of their lives. The characters are made up of an ensemble of traits taken from many different girls that I've encountered over the years.

The story is based around two unlikely friends who create an extraordinary bond to meet a common goal—to get out of the life of escorting. They both navigate the dark world of sex, drugs, money, violence and treachery.

I have a daughter to whom this book is dedicated; I certainly would not want this for her or anyone else's daughter. I hope to paint such a dark portrait over the sex industry that this book may discourage young women from entering into it. It may possibly even persuade women that are already in the sex industry to look at alternatives other than selling their bodies.

I would like to apologize in advance to my mother and sister Lesah for some of the graphic language and scenarios in this book. I cringe at the thought of exposing this side of my past to you guys. Thank you Lesah for all your edification and divine vision; genius is having the ability to see something in the mind's eye. Most people can't see anything until it's in the physical world. You are certainly pure genius and love.

# CONTENTS

# 1

# BAIL MONEY

"Life without service to others is not a life worth living."

I was really trying to understand why I was getting dressed at three-thirty in the morning, getting out of a warm bed next to this sexy chocolate vixen. If I said I was mad that would be an understatement. *What makes this bitch think she should call me, of all people to come and bail her out of jail—like I'm fucking her or something!*

As I sat on the edge of the bed tying the laces on my shoes, I felt my night guest stir from underneath the covers. With a voice as soft as her touch she asked, "Baby where are you going?"

Without even looking up from my shoes, my voice still husky from sleep, I answered, "I'm asking myself that same question too Mama, go back to sleep. I'll be back shortly." I exited out my kitchen door into the garage and watched the automatic garage door open slowly. The humid Decatur air rushed into the garage. It would take me twenty minutes to get downtown. Although Atlanta had become known for its notorious traffic and non-drivers, I-20 would be clear this time of morning.

I've always been a sucker for a tearful female. Her pleas on the other line left me with no choice. In between some sobbing, sniffling and a few audible words that I managed to piece together, I was able to gather that she was indeed locked up and needed me to come down to Fulton County and get her out of jail. All of this was squeezed into a three-minute phone conversation before I heard the operator say, "You have thirty seconds before your call is ended." I heard her blurt out a few more words then the phone went dead.

I really did not mind putting the money up to get her out because I had every intention of getting my money back from her. My real issue was signing my government name on any bonding papers. Furthermore, I had no idea exactly what she had been charged with. Curiosity was getting the best of me. I was certain that she did not go out on a call or at least not a call that I sent her on.

From day one I knew this was not the life for Tamika. I certainly did my personal best to shield and deter her from ever getting into this business. These young chicks watch too much BET. Microwave success seems to be the theme out here in Atlanta or many urban cities for that matter. Everybody wants to live the fabulous life. I've heard Atlanta referred to as Black Hollywood, although the most accurate adjective would be Never-Neverland. Yeah, Never-Neverland would be way more appropriate since no one ever has to grow up here. This is a city where thirty-something-year-old females still show up on music video sets to get a cameo in their favorite rapper's video. Despite all of that, I actually love this city. Like most people here, I'm a transplant myself. Atlanta has all four seasons with little to no snow. What is there not to love about that!

I pulled up into a parking spot right in front of the bail bondsman's door, which was located directly across from the Fulton County Jail. The ride downtown had calmed me down considerably. I walked in, filled out the necessary paperwork, gave the slow-ass sixty-something-year-old guy my credit card and walked back out to my vehicle to start the long wait. The wheels of justice were slow.

Truth of the matter was that I did care about Tamika's well-being—I did from the very start. I did know, however, that I could not throw on a cape every time one of these hoes had a personal crisis. I mean at any time of the month we could have a roster of twenty to thirty girls on call. Yeah, that's thirty different personalities, thirty different premenstrual syndromes (PMS), and thirty different issues that really didn't have any bearing on my life at all. Over time I had learned to detach emotionally from anything that did not have to do with the bottom line of the agency. This was much more of a task for me seeing that it went against my natural caring spirit. Tamika was really my own redemption; wanting to save her was sincerely a measure of my own selfishness. I just wanted to right a few of my wrongs. It had nothing to do with the charity of my heart. Sitting in my truck, looking at the evolving justice system from my viewpoint, I could surmise what people's charges were as they made the required bail. I watched a young teenage boy being chastised by his mother as they walked out of the jail—possibly some sort of petty robbery or assault charge. If history repeats itself it probably wouldn't be the last time she would have to come get her son out of there. Damn, it's amazing how these young boys let their pants hang so low off their waists without falling completely down. It has to be some sort of art form at this point because it has to take skills to do that. What I was watching had to be late night or early morning entertainment at its best, depending on your point of view. A red candy-color Cadillac with rims pulled up and blew its fancy-sounding air horn that seemed to play a short tune. On cue, two scantily-clothed young ladies ran out to the car. The clicking of their high heels on the sidewalk echoed in the early morning air. As they jumped into the Caddy, it was apparent that they were met with a verbal lashing. Homeboy's arms were flaring up and down as the car rocked back and forth from his excitement. He was certainly an animated character. Daddy was not happy! Did this dude have a perm in his hair? Only in the south would you see some shit like this—this day and age homeboy got a perm! I was glad that I had live entertainment because it took my mind off of the long wait as well as what awaited me back home in my warm bed. I had gotten over my initial anger over the wee hour phone call. A sense of civic duty came across me as I laughed to myself. *What's our purpose out here if we can't help a cause greater than our own, right!* There's no feeling like being in jail thinking nobody cares about you. I've been there. This was about me balancing out the universe. God knows I've put my share of bullshit into the atmosphere.

I must have dozed off because I woke up to the tapping of the bail bondsman's ring finger at my driver's side window. "Hey they just released her. She's on her way down."

"Thanks! What door will she come out of?"

He gestured to the same door everyone had been exiting all morning. I guess I was still a bit discombobulated from my snooze. I sat up straight and reached into my arm console to grab my spare trial-size bottle of mouthwash. After I gargled and spit outside the window, I felt fully revived. The paperwork with Tamika's charges was very vague as to the details of her arrest. It simply read, "Assault" but who, what, when and how was the question. Tamika, like most young girls in the 'hood, grew up without a father in a rough side of Atlanta. I liked her and found her very attractive from day one. I kept it totally professional, never letting on to the desire that she did stir up in me. She was driven and determined more than any other girl I had seen come through the agency. She talked about getting her own place and car in a matter-of-fact kind of way, only to look up and she had gotten herself a condo in Atlantic Station, just like she said she would. Then I got that call, "Czar I won't need you to drive me anymore. I just copped that convertible Mercedes CLK. And to think you didn't want to hire me, huh." She was so happy with her own accomplishment. For the first time in her twenty-one years on this earth, she was not living in poverty—at least not physical poverty. Is there a moral poverty? Who was I to judge any of these girls? Did the ends justify the means! I couldn't answer that either way.

I looked up through the front windshield window to see a female figure that sort of looked like Tamika. I had not physically seen her in a few weeks. I booked her calls on the phone and she usually made her drops while I was out of the office. I didn't know if she was purposely avoiding me but I was a bit too busy to really notice.

I had heard whispers and gossip about Tamika's alleged drug use and drinking. All these hoes did was talk so you couldn't separate facts from fiction sometimes. I guess I did not want to think the worst but from my point-of-view, looking through my window, she was nothing but a shell of that pretty, sexy, next-door-type beauty I had first met. I blew my horn to get her attention. She seemed startled and very much shaken by the sound of the horn. I revved the engine to drive across the street to her but she was already making her way to me. She ran across the street wearing rubber flip-flops. It was obviously her as she got closer and closer. I reached over my middle console to push open the passenger door and let her in.

I was not ready for what happened next. Tamika got into the car and I saw something in her eyes that I had never seen nor expected to see from her—FEAR. That sassy, slick mouth was mute and quivering. At first my focus was fixated on Tamika's sullen face. As my eyes traveled down to her shirt, I noticed the blood stains all over her. Before I could ask any questions, Tamika totally fell apart. I reached over to embrace her in my arms. She was crying her eyes out and I could feel the tears soaking my shoulder through my shirt. I usually could muster up words of encouragement but I had nothing. She just wanted and needed to be held at that moment. I had worked so hard to distance my emotions from most of these girls. This type of vulnerability from Tamika was so far from the Tamika I had known; I was simply stunned. I would later understand that her tears were not about her arrest but all the choices that had led up to it. As we sat there hugged up to each other, I even began questioning my life choices. It had been in the making for a few months now. This was just the springboard to give it serious consideration. It was times like this that a square mundane life didn't seem so bad. A regular nine-to-five may not be exciting or fulfilling but it was safe. Maybe I needed to start on my two-point-five kids and white picket fence with a dog. Who was I kidding? That's not who I am. The thought fled as fast as it had entered my mind. I would probably lose my mind after a month or so of a nagging wife censoring my every move. I attempted to push away from Tamika's grasp, only to be pulled closer and tighter. I understood at that moment that she just needed to be held and nothing more. I decided not to pry for any answers to my numerous questions and just be.

The sun was coming up by the time I pulled out of the bondsman's parking lot. Tamika had settled down a whole lot. She still had not spoken one word to me. My questions would have to wait. Where was the blood from? Why did she have bandages on her forearms? Who was involved? Where did this happen? I looked over at her curled up on the passenger seat with her knees to her chest, eyes closed. Yeah, I knew that feeling. If we could just sleep away some of the problems of life, huh! I jumped on the highway headed north on I-75/85 and exited on Seventeenth Street, making the left at the ramp and pulling in front of Tamika's building. I really had to hesitate before waking her up. I knew this was some of the best sleep she had had in the last couple of hours.

I reached over and shook her gently. "Hey, Tamika. Tamika, wake up. We're here."

She poked her head up to see that we were parked in front of her building instead of her parking garage deck. She looked at me and spoke for the first time in a real faint voice. "Please stay with me." It was not a question but instead came across more as a deep plea.

"Sure." It just came out.

She grabbed my hand and gently squeezed it in appreciation. I pulled around to the garage then up to her level. We walked arm in arm to her condo. I reminded myself that I would have to call my house guest and tell her to let herself out. I wouldn't be back in time.

As soon as we entered Tamika's place I immediately went to the bathroom and ran her a hot bath. I then returned to the kitchen and put the kettle on to boil, for some soothing green tea. Tamika just stood there as if she was in a stranger's house. I took her by the hand and led her into her bedroom. I helped her out of her clothes exposing the bruises and marks that were on her neck and down her back. She stood naked with her hands dropped to her sides. Her shoulders were hunched over. Her eyes were lifeless. Tamika looked completely broken. I looked at her naked body and for the first time I saw her for what she was. She was a lost, twenty-one-year-old that never had a chance to be a little girl. She'd been on her own from the tender age of fourteen. She was sexually molested too many times by too many different people to remember. She never knew her father and her mother's drug addiction took precedence over the rearing of her. That hard persona that I knew and saw was completely gone. She must have seen what I just saw as she looked in her mirror. She broke out crying again with her arms outstretched for me to hold her. I complied and held her like a sister.

After a minute or two I picked up the pile of bloody clothes and placed them in the garbage. I walked her to the now hot tub of bubbles in the bathroom. She tested the temperature with the big toe of her left foot then climbed in and sat flat. I returned to the kitchen and made two cups of green tea, sweetened with honey. I brought her her cup while she soaked in the tub. I took my tea and walked through the living room, out onto the balcony. I loved this view of the city's skyline; it was actually growing more and more every day. This was such a reflective moment for me. I could not help but think of how hard I had tried to keep Tamika out of the industry. Maybe I saw who she truly was back then—Little Miss Persistent. What more could I have done to prevent her from being in this situation right now? Let me share how Tamika and I first met.

# 2
# NIGHTLIFE

"True happiness is not an exterior occasion or event;
happiness works from the inside out."

I love driving up Peachtree Street. Maybe it's because I'm a native New Yorker, one of the largest metropolises in the world, and this strip of clustered buildings and busy pedestrians offers me a sense of home. I was in the moment, absorbing the whole scene of Atlanta's night life. Shout was on my right, with that yellow and red neon sign that was so inviting, and that line of sexy hard-bodies—females ready to burn off some tension of the work week they just got through. They were ready to throw back a few apple martinis and flirt with a few of ATL's getting-money dudes. Mix that with the motorcade of luxury cars at the valet. And when I say luxury, I mean young cats coming through in Bentleys, 550 Benz's, big SUV's with rims that had these chickenhead's heads spinning. We continued north on Peachtree going past Intermezzo, Benihana and Justin on the left. Monday nights were still popping over there at Justin's. I began to relax as we got closer to our destination.

My passenger, Beverly, was a twenty-five-year-old honey-complexioned beauty transplant from Chicago. She was five-foot-ten, one hundred fifty-pounds, 34D-26-36, with hazel eyes, long sandy brown hair, full pouty lips and an angelic voice. How did I know her measurements so well for a man? Especially for a man that was not hers? Simple, I'd heard her give that same exact description of herself dozens of times over the phone to prospective clients—johns, tricks, whatever you want to call them. You see, we were working, or let me rephrase that, she was working and for a fifty dollar driving fee, I was her hoe for one hour. I made sure she got where she needed to go and no harm came to her in the process. We made the left on Pharr Road then another at a stop sign and drove about three hundred feet only to dead-end into the luxurious Concord high-rise condominiums. As we pulled up, we went around the circular driveway with the huge water fountain in the center with its cascading waterfall and its lights shimmering through the water. It was rumored that the least expensive two bedroom condo in this place was like four hundred thousand dollars, and that was in this down market.

Just as I stopped in front of the entrance Beverly shut the overhead vanity light and flipped the sun visor back up, putting away the last of her make-up. She looked up, smiling at me with her doe eyes, and with real confidence, asked, "How do I look?"

"Like somebody about to make some money," I replied.

With that she grinned and nodded in agreement then opened the door to let herself out. "I'll call you when I'm checking in."

"Okay, I'll be down here."

"Don't you leave. I'm going to be in and out."

"You talking like you got some super coochie."

"You don't know nigga?" She shut the door behind her and turned around to walk up the steps into the building. It was not until that very moment I realized why pimps or men of leisure as they are known, called the hoe stroll, "the track." She looked like a gracious stallion just strutting her stuff, as if in slow motion. Her tights and calves looked so muscular and toned but very feminine. The four-inch stilettos she wore hiked up the rear of her already short skirt. She could be anybody's girlfriend, wife, lover, you name it. And for the right price I guess she was. Just before entering the doorway, she flashed a big bright glance in my direction, with a flirtatious smile. I crinkled my eyebrows and shot her back a *girl stop playing* look. With that she disappeared behind the door.

I'd been driving escorts for about two years by now. At first it just supplemented my income, and what man doesn't want to be around a bunch of fine freaks and make money at the same time? As I learned more about the business I was given a management position, which entailed me being in the office, on the phones booking calls, hiring models, and interacting with the publications in which we advertised. The office was where I was glad I was not tonight. Fridays in Buckhead were live as hell. When I first moved to Atlanta, it was a majority of white people partying in Buckhead but now it was the opposite. I guess Memorial Drive and Bankhead (not to be confused with Buckhead) were not good enough for the niggas. On this day it was predominantly black partygoers out here. I pulled up in a vacant spot between a G-500 Benz truck and a Maserati. *Shit!* I thought as I smiled to myself. *I know she got to come back downstairs with a big-ass tip, with whips like this out here, I know it!*

My phone began to ring and I answered, "Hello?"

"I'm checking in," Beverly's voice replied.

"Okay, I got you down at 10:17 P.M."

"Okay."

A check-in served many purposes, the first and most important, to let the trick, excuse me, the client know, that someone knew where the model was, and secondly it told me that the girl had the money in her hand and everything was cool. This was actually the hard part of my job, just waiting for the girl to be done with the session. I stopped the engine, turned the radio down low, reclined the power seats and layed back to wait for that check-out call. Just as I was slipping comfortably into a light sleep, the vibration of my cell woke me up. Looking down at it, I could see the word *Office* illuminated on the face of the phone. What the hell did they want?

"Hello."

"What's up Czar?"

"Nothing, just waiting for Beverly to check out of her call. You got something else working for her after this?"

"I may." Tee was in the office manning the phone switchboard tonight. What that meant was that she would keep me busy making money all night. Tee ran the agency and did a real good job at doing so. What I could not understand was how she got into this somewhat sordid business at all. She had grown up in Alabama, graduated from Tuskegee University and from what I heard, her family was well-off. Tee was very attractive but she downplayed her appearance, possibly on purpose. Even so, I saw how those double-D's hung on her slender five-foot-eight frame, despite all the baggie clothes she wore. She kept her smooth caramel-complexioned face, camouflaged with teacher's glasses. That was the way she came through, real plain Jane like. She could by far be her own top model at the agency, but I think she had bigger plans in mind. I had too much respect for her to try and hit it, plus that would have messed up my money one way or the other in the long run. Business and pleasure rarely ever worked out.

"Czar, I want you to give this potential model a call and run down the criteria to work with the agency. She's been calling for the last three days."

"What's her background Tee?"

"I really did not get all those details. Every time she called I was too busy booking clients."

"Okay, I'll follow up on her."

"Thanks Czar. I don't know what I'd do without you."

"Peace."

I had barely hung up with Tee when my phone jolted me with a buzzing vibration which startled me. I looked down to see the name *Beverly* lit up on the face of the screen.

"Hello, what's up!"

"Beverly, checking out."

"Okay, I'm down in front waiting. Come on Ma." *Damn, 10:57 P.M. Maybe she does have some super coochie,* I thought to myself. I reached over to my left door panel and pressed the number 1 preset seat position. The seat automatically adjusted to my custom posture which sat me up in driving position. I turned the key, revved the engine up, backed out of the spot and pulled around to the front of the building. Right on cue, Beverly walked out the front door, her face looking a little flushed, her hair still immaculate except for a few wayward strands. From the smirk that she was giving me from the top of the steps, I could tell she got that big tip I knew she was going to get. When she opened the passenger door it illuminated the interior of the truck for about five seconds until she hopped up and closed the door behind her. Before we could exchange any words she was slapping greenbacks into the palm of my hand just the way I liked it. There was the regular fifty dollar driving fee and a little something extra for me.

Beverly was a driver's ideal type of model. She took precise, accurate directions, never touched anything in my car including my radio and she was just all around pleasant to be around. We would occasionally catch a movie or go out to eat in between calls and she never had any reservation about paying for it all; I really dug her. Beverly was a full time student at Spelman College, majoring in economics. She was an above average student and she was very determined to succeed. I drove dozens upon dozens of females for the service but there was definitely something different about Beverly. You have females in the business who have been sexually abused by older males in their family or even by their own fathers. You have the ones who have *special management*, otherwise known as pimps. You have the single mothers who are just trying to keep a roof, food and some clothes on their children's back. Don't let me forget the down-low, in the closet, crackheads, weedheads, ecstasy pill poppers, and the powder snorters who have other motivators in their systems. Beverly was none of the above. She went to a very exclusive private school up until she came to Spelman here in Atlanta. Her diction was articulate and professional. Maybe that was why those white tricks took to her the way they did. Whatever it was, it translated into more money in my pocket and that was always a good thing.

"Yo Ma, Tee may have another call for you."

"Okay, that's what's up then."

At about five o'clock—four calls later and a couple of hundred dollars richer—my cohort of the night, Beverly, and I decided to call it a night (or a morning, depending on your point of view).

"Yo Ma, are you up to taking another call?"

"No, just take me home. I'm tired as hell."

"Okay, let me call Tee and let her know that we are calling off and won't be available until later."

I dialed the agency and Tee picked up the phone on the second ring with the same amount of enthusiasm as she did in the earlier part of our night. "Tee, what's up, it's Czar. Me and Beverly are calling off. I got her agency fees but I'm too tired to come out to the office now so I'll settle up with you later."

"That's cool Czar."

"Aight, peace."

"Yo Czar, don't hang up. You there?"

"Yeah, go ahead Tee."

"Before I forget, give that young lady a call—the one I mentioned who was interested in working."

"She called back again?"

"Yes, again. She most certainly did."

"Well, if we hire her I guess we can use Miss Persistent as her stage name." Tee and I laughed in agreement and with that we said good night, or in this case, good morning, and hung up.

After dropping Beverly off I could not help but wonder how happy she was doing this. This question was taboo in the business, nonexistent really, but I suspected it was on all the girls' minds when they were home alone. It certainly was on mine. Making money was voiced as a justification but I felt otherwise. True happiness is not an exterior occasion or event. Happiness works from the inside out.

# 3
# TURNED OUT

"Learn from others' mistakes.
You don't have enough time to make them all yourself."

The beginning of the week is usually slow for agencies. Everybody is just winding down from the weekend and falling back into their routine of life. I was no exception to this as I straightened up the house and did some laundry while I had the time. Going through the pockets of a dirty pair of jeans I was about to place into the washing machine, I came across a piece of paper with a phone number and the name Tamika on it. *Tamika… Tamika… who the hell is Tamika?* I repeated the name in an attempt to jar my memory. I hate when I can't place a name with a number or face. Then it dawned on me this was little Miss Persistent, the potential model that was relentless in her efforts to join the agency. With such tenacity I wondered why she couldn't find a regular job. I had scribbled the name and number down the previous night after talking to Tee.

*It's Monday. I ain't doing shit. Why not check out some fresh new ass,* I thought to myself. After cleaning up and getting everything together, I took out the small piece of paper that was crinkled up in my pocket. I unfolded it and dialed the numbers, 404-555-6928. *Damn, I should have dialed *67 to block my* *number. I don't need no jealous boyfriend or concerned parent calling me about their "precious" little girl.* Before I could hang up and redial the number with the appropriate *67 prefix, little Miss Persistent was on the other end. "Hello? Heellooo, are you there?"

"Yeah, sorry about that. I'm Czar. You called our agency in reference to a job."

"Hi, I'm Tamika. I've been calling and calling. Thank you for finally getting back at me."

"No problem Ma. Tamika, what we do is an initial phone interview where I ask you a few questions and tell you the criteria to work with our agency then you get an opportunity to ask some questions. How does that sound?"

"That's fine."

"Okay, let's get started. First and far most importantly how old are you?"

"Twenty-one."

"Twenty-one!"

"Yeah, don't you have to be at least eighteen to work for a strip club or an escort service in the state of Georgia?"

"Well yeah, do you have a state ID showing that you're twenty-one?"

"Of course I do."

"Give me a brief description of yourself."

"Well, I'm five-foot-eight, one hundred forty pounds, 34C-32-36. That's a full C cup I might add," she said, snickering. "I have a short Halle Berry style haircut, high cheekbones, and light brown eyes. I almost forgot my washboard abs and my tight little wet pussy! Is that enough of a description for you?" She was being facetious.

I just ignored her last comment and went on with my questioning as if I never heard her, thinking to myself, *slick mouth huh, I got something for that mouth. These little bitches think they are so grown.* "Have you ever worked in adult entertainment before?"

"NO."

"Never?"

"Nope."

Damn, personally at this point I had already made up my mind not to hire Miss Twenty-one-year-old, persistent Tamika. I had rules. I wasn't going to be responsible for any turnouts. Not on my watch. What's a turnout you ask? Well a turnout is the pride and joy of any agency or pimp. It's a fresh new face that has never sold their body before. Pimps wear a new turnout like it's some sort of feather in their crown. But for me a turnout was an opportunity to right some of my wrongs or set some of my bad karma right if you will. Even when I was in the drug game in my late teens and early twenties, I never gave any work to some kid that still was in school and had a chance at being something more. I just never wanted to street poison anyone plain and simple. Once that poison pill is swallowed there's no turning back. One taste of some fast money and it's pretty much a wrap. You ultimately are holding someone's hand while you lead him or her straight to hell, and I was not about to do that. These were my rules. Today these young kids have absolutely no rules at all.

At this juncture I was thinking of a way I could make the escorting industry sound as unappealing as possible so that twenty-one year old, Miss Persistent, Tamika, would reconsider her employment options when I got done. I'd make flipping burgers sound real enticing by the time I was finished. Waiting tables at Gladys's would seem like a luxury when I finished painting this picture.

"Well Tamika, what makes you think you can handle being an escort?"

With a whole lot of attitude, she replied, "Look, I'm a freak and I like money. Does that answer your question?"

"It's a lot more to it than being a freak and liking money, shorty. What happens when you get a call and you have to go fuck and suck some three hundred pound guy? His weight and size makes it hard to clean his self properly."

"Does he have his money correct, Czar? Yeah, well I'll be sucking on his dick then won't I!! Look Czar I'm about my money."

"What about female clients?" I asked with a big grin. I knew I was going to snob her with that question or so I thought.

"Shit, I fuck with females on and off in my personal life anyway. I'd rather do more female calls if possible. Can you arrange that?" Tamika continued, "Have you not heard of the term Gay for Pay?"

*Damn I'm out of touch with things.* When I was in my teens there was no homosexual or lesbianism around my peers growing up. At this point I had to just go for the gusto. "Tamika, you really think you're ready for this business, huh?"

"Hell yeah!!"

"Do you realize that you may have a client that wants to put a twelve-inch dick up your ass? Can you handle an anal situation? What about a client that gets two or three of his boys and they want to gangbang you, huh? Are you still down, to 'get your money' as you put it? Or maybe you have the stomach to fuck a man in his ass with a huge strap-on dildo. If you're still unfazed, how about the reality of going to jail? How does jail sound to you? Or even worse, what if one of these deranged muthafuckers snaps and cuts your throat, ear to ear, leaving you in a pool of your own blood to die?"

There was nothing but silence on the phone. I had been successful for sure. Her silence spoke volumes. After my long spiel, Tamika nonchalantly spoke in the calmest, most unemotional tone I'd ever heard. "Listen I can show you way better than I can tell you. Does this conclude this portion of the interview?"

*Smart mouth little bitch!* I really did not know what else to say other than, "Do you have any questions for the agency?"

"No, I'm just ready to get it popping."

"Get it popping, huh? Okay. I'll give you a call to come out so we can physically take a look at you in person to determine if you have a marketable look and go into some more details of employment that could not be discussed over the phone. How does that sound?"

"Now that's what's up," she replied with glee in her voice. "When can I expect to hear from you Czar?"

"I'll give you a call and get some directions to your location. What area do you live in?"

"West End shawty, you already know!" The enthusiasm in her voice told me she was totally committed to going all the way through with her newfound hazardous occupation. Did she even view it as hazardous? Little did she know, my campaign to derail her was far from over. I personally had so many questions. Where were her parents? What was her educational level? Why was she not giving herself other options? Ordinarily I'd let a hoe be a hoe, but where do we draw the line? I guess I was strapping on my Captain Save-a-Hoe cape for Tamika, a bit taken aback by the all so fresh conversation I just had with her. I thought to myself, this would be my personal crusade. Call me Captain Save-a-Hoe if you want, but there was something inside my spirit that told me it was definitely the right thing to do in this case and that was enough for me.

Far too many times I'd seen young girls get into the business thinking that they'd escort long enough to just pay some bills off, get a car or a place of their own but before they know it two to three years have passed and they're doing the same thing. That whole thing about dancing and escorting to pay school tuition is a fallacy. There are very few girls in the sex industry that are actually "paying their way through school." We should have a whole lot more female brain surgeons and doctors running around here, shouldn't we, as much as these chicks be in the clubs popping their kitties in Atlanta. Fast money is addictive and even more dangerous to one's work ethic. It's easy to develop the "I don't really have to work for what I want" mentality. No good can ever come from it. This was not for Little Miss Persistent and I was going to make sure of it!

While in the office with Tee on Tuesday morning as if on cue, without even a good morning, she asked, "Have you interviewed Tamika as yet?"

I began talking to myself, *Come up with an excuse. Come up with an excuse.* "Tee, I don't think shorty going to work out with what we got going here. I did the phone interview and she just doesn't articulate well. I think she'll blow the call before she could even book it. She a bit too 'hood, Tee. You know these upscale clients don't want a 'hood rat from the West End showing up at their door. And not to mention she don't even have her own transportation."

"Czar, I spoke to Tamika and I actually was impressed with her diction. Why do you think I've been on you about getting her on board so hard? Not to mention, she's brand new to the business—fresh meat! She comes without those bad hoe habits. I stand behind my decision to bring her on board and place her on the on call list. And since when have you had a problem hiring a model without a car? It sounds like some driving fees in it for you! I want her signed on and taking calls by Thursday." As she walked out of the door, she added, "We have a big weekend coming up."

At the end of the day this was Tee's show and I was quite aware as to what side of the toast my bread was buttered on. Oh well, the road to hell is paved with good intentions. I heard the door slam as I mumbled, "Okay Tee. I'll get on it."

After paying some of the monthly publications that we advertised our full page ads in, I fiddled around and procrastinated as long as I possibly could before picking up the phone to call Tamika/Lil Miss Persistent.

"Hey Tamika, how are you doing?"

With that now familiar glee in her voice, she responded, "I'm doing well. I see you calling to put a bitch on huh!"

"Yeah, I'm calling to get directions so I can 'put a bitch on.'"

She ignored my sarcasm-laced mocking of her response. "Czar I see I'm going to have to give you some of this good, good because you seem to be way too serious for this job," she said, laughing on the other line as I just shook my head. *This chick is a trip, I can already tell!* "Okay, you come I-20 East, get off on Lee Street. You make a left on the ramp and come down, go past the West End Mall on the right and cross over Ralph

David Abernathy. Go past the West End train station on the left, then on the second street before the railroad tracks, make that right and come down like about two hundred feet and park on the left. I'll come out. How long will it take you to get here?"

"I'm coming from Buckhead so like about fifteen or twenty minutes. You know how unpredictable Atlanta traffic is."

"Okay, see you then! What will you be driving?"

"A black SUV."

"I'll be ready and looking out."

"Cool."

It was still early noon when I pulled up in front of her place. The early traffic was kind to me. As if she anticipated my arrival, the door opened up before I could put the car into park. I looked over my left shoulder through the much too dark driver side front window. I had to put the window down to take her all in. Wow! That's the body attached to that smart mouth—five-foot-eight, one hundred forty pounds, never looked so damn good.

Over the phone, most potential models exaggerated their looks. When asked to rate themselves on a scale of one to ten, the popular answer was always, "I'm at least a nine, for real. Come see. You'll hire me on the spot." But in this case, Tamika was honestly very modest.

Her statement about her tight little wet pussy came back to my mind; I was inclined to believe her. I put the thought out of my head as she approached the truck. As she got closer I gestured to her with my head motion to get in on the passenger side. She had on a colorful turquoise and lavender knee-length sundress. It was no doubt from the Bebe design collection. After being around females as much and as long as I have, fragrances, designers and shoes became very familiar to me. She bounced into the front seat smiling, playfully punching me in the arm.

"You're way too handsome to be always acting so mean on the phone, Czar. I'm finally glad to put a face with the voice."

Without cracking a smile or showing any sort of emotions, I extended my hand to give her a business-style handshake, introducing myself. "Well, I must admit you have a marketable appearance Tamika."

"Did you have any doubt?"

"I always have doubt, babe. First things first, let me see your ID. I have to confirm your age before I can have any kind of adult discussion businesswise with you."

"Sure." She ruffled through her matching spaghetti strap bag to produce her driver's license.

"Okay, July 12, huh? That's right around the corner." Yeah! I made a mental note that she was a Cancer like myself. It was late May meaning Memorial Weekend was coming up fast.

Sitting there looking right into her eyes I could smell the naiveté all over her. Even though it was silent in the car, I tumultuously wrestled with myself on the inside. Her words broke my trance.

"What's next?"

I thought to myself, *my thoughts exactly!* Her words gave me one last ditch effort attempt to sway her in the opposite direction of her current aspirations. Our agency's reputation preceded us in many ways but none more than our notorious "courtesy calls." A courtesy call was really simple. When a secretary goes out for a job she has to prove she can type forty words per minute, right? Police and firemen have to take physical tests to prove they can do the job right? Well, this was no different. We were hiring whores so they too had to prove that they could do the job. We had a whole orientation like any Fortune 500 company would before bringing on an employee. The orientation was what governed us and gave each model an even playing field in the agency. My plan was really simple. After she filled out her paperwork and was briefed on the rules during orientation, I would have two guys on standby to pound her little ass out during her courtesy call. This was Little Miss Persistent's ass *literally*. I smiled at the thought of telling Tee, "She just changed her mind about escorting." Check mate!

I pulled off and headed back through downtown on our way back to the office. I made the two necessary phone calls to pull off my special courtesy call for our persistent friend in my passenger seat. Derrick and Malik were more than happy to get an unexpected call to fuck some new pussy. While both men tried to draw me into giving a detailed description of their target, I had to cut them both short since she was sitting immediately to the right of me within earshot. I summed it up as, "She straight," hanging up on them. We made small talk on the way back to the office. I flashed my gate card while coming through the gated community where our office was housed.

"Wow this is nice."

"Yeah, you're not in the West End anymore, huh!"

"Yeah, very funny."

I pulled up to the door entrance as Kevin the valet rushed over. "Hey Czar, what's up?"

"I'm cool man."

"You want me to leave you up front or take you down into the garage?"

"You can leave it here and leave the keys in it."

"Okay."

We stepped onto the gleaming marble vestibule, walked in past the front desk, greeted security and the concierge. "Hey Czar, we see you working brother! We see you working! Always working!"

Tamika was acting like a real never-see come-see. She touched the exotic flower arrangement to see if it was real. "Damn, I never saw real flowers that look so pretty before. They looked fake but when I touched them, I could tell they were real."

"I know babe, I know."

We got on the elevator. The doors shined so brightly that they clearly reflected our images back at us. Enough so that Tamika needed to comment on it. "Damn, they must clean these every day."

We exited on the nineteenth floor and headed to number 1904, the corner unit.

As I turned the knob and key simultaneously to enter into the plush condo/office, Tamika was right on my heels. This corner unit afforded us way more space and much more natural sunlight. I turned around to see a speechless wide-eyed, open mouth Tamika gazing in awe of the place. "Man, rent here must be like thirteen hundred dollars or more huh!?"

"Nah, that's just the HOA fees."

Tamika quizzically asked, "What does HOA stand for?"

"It's the homeowners association. We pay them for the upkeep and the dozens of amenities that this building offers."

"Ameni-- what?"

"Try the monthly mortgage being six thousand a month!"

"Czar, that's my whole year's rent in one month. What the fuck took you so long to come hire me Czar? Shit I need to be living like this," she stated, still taking in everything with her eyes and a bewildered look across her face.

It was so obvious that I had my work cut out for me. That saying ignorance is bliss was so, so true in this case right in front of me. I contemplated for a while and the silence of the condo gave me clarity. I had this Ah Ha Moment. I would take a softer, more tactful approach to discouraging Tamika from taking that pill—that street poison pill that's so hard to turn back from. "Hey, Tamika, why don't you take a seat?"

She sat directly opposite me as she flopped down on the contemporary coffee-colored leather sectional. The light-colored hardwood floor glimmered brightly with the marriage of the midday sunlight. The balcony blinds drawn open, invited the city into our conversation. From her expressionless look, it was understood we were about to have a heartfelt conversation. "Tamika, why do you want to be an escort?"

"I think it's very obvious, why."

"I guess what I'm trying to say is have you explored your other options?"

"What other options? Fucking McDonalds or maybe in a mall doing retail for a bunch of ungrateful customers? No thank you."

"I mean you're twenty-one years old. That's what a twenty-one-year-old does. You should be thinking about college right now. Did you finish high school?"

"I got my G.E.D."

"Where do you see yourself five years from now Tamika?"

"Look Czar, I'm just happy to be here and to have made it this far. I've lived in every slum Atlanta has to offer, Herdon Homes, Simpson Road, Fourth Ward, so yes, the West End is a come up for me. I'm a product of a junkie-ass mother and a sperm donating muthafucking father. I've been in and out of foster homes all of my life. I can't even count the number of times I've been molested and had no one to go to. I'm out here in this world by myself, do you understand that. By myself! I see the nice ride you pulled up in." Flaring her hands upwards, she continued, "What, you going to let me live here?!" I sat silently trying to hold back the pain I felt for this young girl, or so I thought. "I have nobody but me. I have to do what I have to do." At this point her arms folded and she hunched over, shaking back and forth with tears streaming down her young pretty face, murmuring, "I have nobody, nobody," faintly to herself.

I got up, walked to the bathroom and turned on the cold water. My hands transformed into a bowl that I filled with water then splashed my face. I was not hot. I just wanted to mask my tears with some water. I composed myself, drying my face and hands then walked over to the kitchen, retrieving two bottles of water from the refrigerator. I offered one to Tamika and sat back down across from her taking a sip from mine. Holding her head down and avoiding eye contact, she said, "I'm sorry. I did not mean for all that to come out." Her voice cracked between tears. "It's just my reality. It's just my reality right now."

I reached over and grabbed the box of Kleenex, handing it to her. She reached over and grabbed it, mustering up a smile and starting to compose herself. At that one moment I saw so much strength in that young girl it was amazing. She now sat up, legs crossed, hand-in-hand on her knees, looking me squarely in the face. "I'm ready to start the orientation whenever you are Czar."

Before I could even respond, the ring of my cell phone broke the silence. I grabbed it to see the name Tee flashing back at me. What the fuck, did she have a camera on me. Her timing was uncanny. "Hey Tee what's popping?"

"Hey Czar, I was just checking in on you."

"Yeah!"

"By the way, have you seen the new model yet?"

"It's funny that you ask. I have her at the office right now about to fill out her application and do her orientation."

"Good, good, you know it's Memorial Day weekend coming up so we'll need her on deck ready and on call."

"Okay Tee, talk to you later. She'll be straight."

"That's what I wanted to hear Czar."

After hanging up with Tee it was so evident that I had lost this battle. Had I done everything that I could have? I looked at Tamika then reached into the desk drawer and pulled out our four page application. Really it was three pages and the fourth was a rule sheet. I attach it to a clipboard with a pen, handed it to her then walked over to the ceiling to floor glass door of the balcony. I opened the double glass door and stepped out into the nineteenth floor breeze. I realized that I had to step back into my role on this one. *Put that Captain Save-a-Hoe cape up*, I thought, smiling to myself.

Taking in the view made me see how deceptive Atlanta looked—a lot of luxury high-rises, couture boutiques, and expensive foreign cars, along with patches of greenery everywhere unlike most cities. But beneath it all there was an underbelly of the beast that beats here in this city. They don't call it the Dirty South for nothing. I just hoped that little Miss Persistent didn't meet it. I glanced over my left shoulder to see her feverishly filling out the application. I turned my attention back to the skyline of the city shaking my head thinking, *there's got to be a better way!*

After about five minutes out on the balcony taking in the city, I took a deep breath, and made an about-face to cross the threshold of the door. Tamika looked up, a little startled at my sudden movement. Our eyes locked for a moment, speechless, expressionless. The smirk was now off her face. I mustered up the most assertive tone from the pit of my guts to let her know it was straight business right now. "Aight, I know you're done with that paperwork!"

"Should I sign right here?" she asked, pointing clearly to where it was marked with an X and the word signature.

The look I shot to her communicated all she needed to know. I felt the ice in my veins again. I was totally emotionally removed from this at this point. Who was I to deny a hoe the opportunity to be a hoe! These little bitches were too fast for their own good. I looked at my watch thinking that Derrick and Malik were already en route. *Bitch, I got something for your ass,* I thought to myself. The guys knew the routine. They would get here then text me letting me know that they were waiting in the media room on the first floor. I then, in turn, would text them back with a simple, "Come up," when the application part was coming to a close.

Now, I was sitting directly across from Tamika again with my own copy of the application. "Turn to the first page," I instructed her.

She attempted to ask me a question by raising her hand like we were in school or something. I raised my voice to let her know to put her hand down and let me finish.

"Listen, trust me. I'll get to all your questions. Everything that you signed will be explained in full detail okay?" She shook her head up and down in comprehension.

"Okay, this first page is called the solicitation agreement. This is basically saying that as an agency we discourage any solicitation of money for sex. Listen, after you get the fee from the client, what happens between two adults happens, wink, wink! You understand?"

"Okay, I get it. It's like it's understood huh!"

"Yeah, it's understood babe." What I understood more was with her signature on this legally binding document, any legal issue that could arise with law enforcement, we could pull it out and say, "We told her we don't offer sex. Look, this is her signature right here." And that shit will and does hold up in a court of law.

"Moving on to the second page. This discusses our modeling session or otherwise known as a *courtesy call*. What this is in short is your ability to perform to our standard of expectation in a bedroom situation."

"So what you saying I'll have to fuck somebody."

"Absolutely! Would that be a problem for you?"

"Will I do that today?"

"Yes!"

With a flirtatious grin, she replied, "Yeah, I'm ready for that handsome!"

Naturally she was thinking that since I was the only person currently present, it was going to be with me. I acted like I did not even hear her comment. This visibly annoyed her. One thing that I learned early on in my dealing with attractive women was their massive egos. They've spend so much of their life manipulating men with their sex appeal that without it they were fish out of water. Personally, whenever I'm interested in a woman I totally ignore her. While interacting with her, I don't admit any interest at all. Now she begins asking herself, "Have I lost it? He's not responding the typical way most men do to me." Now she begins to be the pursuer.

We simultaneously turned to the third page in concert with each other. "What we have here is the photo release form. Any pictures and marketing material will be property of the agency. You don't have any problem taking any nude pictures or video that we may post online or in print form, right?"

"No, not at all."

"That's the answer I want to hear, cool. Okay that's pretty straightforward right?"

"Yes it is handsome. Can I get some copies of the pictures?"

"That won't be a problem. Well Tamika, this is the fourth and final page and what I think is the most important part of the orientation. This is called, for lack of a better word, the Rule Sheet. These rules will keep you safe and keep you making money, providing that you follow them! I can't emphasize how pertinent it is that you pay close attention. The last thing I want is some psycho cutting your throat from ear to ear." I saw Tamika take a deep breath then swallow. Visibly shaken, the thought that she could be brutally murdered got her attention. While she sat wide-eyed and quiet, I made a mental note that there was a kink in the armor—Miss Tough Tamika was afraid of the possibility that she could get physically hurt. I suspected it stemmed from the violence and abuse from her past.

She broke her silence to inquire, "Has something like that happened before?"

"Not at this agency, not on my watch. I have heard stories and news reports about other agencies but not here. We do a really great job of screening our clients. For the most part you'll be doing what's called an 'outcall.' This is where you go out to the client's residence or hotel room. Now if you're at someone's home they have way too much to lose in a situation like that, so residential outcalls are ninety-nine percent always good calls.

When you have a hotel outcall you're still very much safe. You figure the client is registered under his name which would connect him to that room if anything were to happen. The second type of call is referred to as an 'incall.' This is where the client meets you at one of our incall locations. We have two other apartments in the city where we have set up incall locations. On a few occasions you may have to get a hotel room and have the client meet you there. So, are you clear on the difference between an outcall and an incall?"

"I am." Her demeanor was a lot more businesslike now. No more innuendos and that stupid smirk was gone. That sassy smart mouth was temporarily on vacation.

"Okay, we have what's called 'checking in and checking out' procedures. That's pretty straightforward. When you get to a client location and he gives you the fee, you then pick up the phone, call the office and give them the exact time that you're about to start your session. This is imperative to your safety. So now we can place you with the client at a particular time and we know what time you should be calling to check out. So we're clear on checking in and checking out?"

"Yeah, I got you Czar."

"Do you have any questions?"

"Yeah, what if the client wants additional time?"

I pointed at her and said, "Excellent question! You'll charge him the rate again and give the office a second call and let them know you'll be staying an additional hour. The office will call your driver to give him the new checkout time. Since we are on the topic of collecting money, it's never a good idea to take your own money into a call. What would be the point in doing that right?!"

"I understand Czar."

"Okay, moving on, we are an escort agency. We don't treat our clients like a car date on Metropolitan Avenue. You're not a street-walker. Eighty-five percent of our clients are repeat, loyal regulars—our bread and butter, very consistent. You're the first line of our customer service. There is a certain attitude that you have to learn here. First off, we don't 'tip hustle.'"

Tamika sat forward, brow wrinkled. "What's that?"

"Tip hustling is asking for additional money after the client has paid the flat fee. As in you telling him well, if you want this, that will be an addition fifty dollars or if you want that it would be an extra sixty dollars. We offer what's referred to as FS or Full Service. Full service consists of a BBBJ and vaginal sex."

"Damn Czar, I hate to sound stupid and keep asking questions but what's a BBBJ?"

"Oh not at all, I want you to ask questions. A BBBJ is an acronym used for bare back blow job. The only time you would charge a client an additional fee is if he requested a 'Greek session.'"

The curl on her lips told me she did not have the slightest idea as to what a "Greek session" was. So I offered without having her ask. "Greek is the term used for anal sex."

"Yuk!" Her eyes widened and her mouth hung open.

"Yeah, are you open for that? No pun intended."

We both laughed before she gave me an, "Of course if I'm going to be paid more."

"Well, all these different terminologies are used to galvanize and encode the fact that we are indeed selling sex. So if you're ever on the phone with a potential client you'll need to know the language as to not incriminate yourself. Okay, you just learned three of the most commonly used terms. I couldn't possibly go over the hundreds that are out there but let's look at some more regularly used ones. You have CIM. You want to take a crack at it?"

Giggling, Tamika responded, "I don't know where to start."

"Take a shot, okay."

"It's 'call in men'? I don't know."

"No, it's actually cum in mouth. Then you have DP which means double penetration of both the vagina and anus simultaneously. Yet another term is GFE which stands for Girlfriend Experience, meaning he may be looking to kiss and have more of an intimate feeling session, more touching and caressing than typical. Here's one, DATY, Dining at the Y, simply put, he wants to eat your pussy. I tell you what. I'll give you a printout of a complete list of terms to learn on your own time."

Tamika said, "Okay, I'll make myself familiar with the whole list of terms."

Looking down at my watch, I knew Derrick and Malik were downstairs patiently waiting for my call. Standing up, I excused myself, reaching for my phone. I dialed Derrick's number. "Hey Derrick, I'm going to be wrapping up in like another ten minutes okay?"

"Cool Czar."

Returning to my seat, I said, "Tamika, I know I'm giving you a lot of information all at once right now but it's necessary."

"That's fine. I'm taking it all in."

"Let's pick up the pace a little bit more okay."

"Sure."

"Proper dress is always casual professional. We don't want you going up into a five-star hotel looking like a street walker."

"You mean like a nice skirt Czar?"

"Yeah and a nice blouse is always a great look. Next, once you call on, you're on. You can't pick and choose what calls you're available for. If you fit the client's criteria I expect you to be going on that call. You cannot differentiate between a Southside call or a call in a downtown hotel. This way there is no preferential treatment among models."

Tamika was nodding in agreement as though she could see how this benefited her. I continued. "Always count your money, make sure it's accurate and not counterfeit. I can't tell you the number of times models try to turn in counterfeit money that was passed to them. I want you to know that if we catch it up here in the office, you still owe us our fee. It's your responsibility to check the money when you get it."

"Well, I'm going to make sure I get a counterfeit marker for their asses."

"That's an excellent idea! Moving on, never rush a client. He's paying for an hour and you're obligated to give him one hour. If you're done with whatever you do in fifteen minutes and he wants to talk baseball or the weather for the next forty-five minutes, that's what he gets, with a smile. Make him believe that you're the biggest baseball fan he ever met. We clear?"

"I totally get it. It's like I'm playing a role for an hour."

"That's an excellent way to view it Tamika. You're role-playing for an hour." With a quick glance at my watch I jumped to the most job-jeopardizing offense—client stealing. Tamika, it's self-explanatory. If you're ever caught giving or taking a client's phone number or seeing them outside of the agency, it's going to be automatic separation. Even though we are in somewhat of a sordid business there should still be a standard of integrity. Our clients are well aware of our policy of never contacting a model directly. I want you to know that we have certain clients that we do ask to attempt to get the new models' numbers. We find out who we can and can't trust very fast. So consider yourself warned. Well, that pretty much sums up that part of the orientation. Oh, one last thing. You're going to be offered all sorts of drugs while you're taking calls. Simply don't do it."

"Czar, I don't even smoke so that should not be a problem for me."

"Good. Don't say I did not warn you. Don't get in over your head babe."

Tamika turned away from my piercing stare. "No, look at me Tamika! DON'T GET IN OVER YOUR HEAD." With that I flashed a smile to cut the tension in the air. Tamika responded with a smile of her own. "Now that that's out of the way, it's time for the courtesy call we discussed earlier."

"That's what I've been waiting for chocolate boy wonder."

"Really cool!" My subtle discrete text to Derrick telling him to head on up with Malik obviously went unnoticed. "Hey Tamika, follow me!" She sprung up from her seat smiling.

We walked down the hall and turned into the first room on the left. We both walked in to be greeted by a queen-size dark wood sleigh bed. The light lavender paint gave the room a very contemporary look. A forty-two-inch flat screen television hung on the wall next to a nightstand with a small exotic potted orchid plant sitting on it. Tamika walked over to the window to take in the view. Her sexy silhouette outlined by the natural light of the sun really showed off her curvaceous figure. *Damn she's a sexy bitch!* I walked over to where she stood. I came up right behind her, peering over her shoulder at the view myself. She said nothing. I felt her motion backwards into my mid-section. She started to gyrate in a circular motion on my now very hard dick. Without turning around she reached for the back of my neck with her right hand pulling my head foreword as to suck on her naked neck. My soft moist lips gently touched her neck once, then twice and then I gently sucked on her neck. Her left hand now traveled down into her own panties. She was massaging her clit slowly and steadily. My left hand held her erect nipple of her left breast between my thumb and index finger. I could now hear the distinct sounds of a mixture of heavy breathing and pleasurable moans. I watched her lips faintly mouth the words, "I want you, I want you. I've wanted you from the first day I saw you."

In one swift movement she turned around and was now on her knees in front of me. Looking up at me, holding and caressing my hard dick through my pants she began reaching for my zipper. I stepped back out of her reach and with my most seductive tone, I told her to get undressed and into the bed. I turned around and walked out, closing the door behind me. I wanted to brief Derrick and Malik before just sending them in the room. I knew that they would be outside the door waiting for me to let them in by now. We had done this dozens of time in the past, sometimes as many as three times in one day. I walked directly to the front door, opening it to Derrick's outstretched hand.

"What's up Czar!" he greeted me, with a big smile on his face as he looked around. Malik was right behind him, greeting me but his eyes were scanning the whole apartment. Simultaneously, they both gave me this quizzical look.

"What shorty look like?" asked Malik.

I huddled closer to the two men and in a hushed voice, answered both of their concerns. "She is fine and sexy as hell. I need ya'll to bang her the fuck out, you understand! I want ya'll to make her reconsider this whole thing, feel me?"

Both men nodded in agreement. We broke up the huddle, composed ourselves and walked to the room. "She's nice, ready and wet too ya'll." I knocked once then pushed the door open to see Tamika sitting up in the bed legs spread open with nothing else on but her high heels. Damn. How did she know about my shoe fetish? The smile that was on her face was extinguished after seeing the two men follow in behind me. "Tamika, this is Derrick." I then motioned to Malik as I mentioned his name. "They will be conducting your courtesy call."

"So what were you? Like the warm up guy!"

I laughed it off without answering her. As I turned around to leave them to their business I could hear Tamika's lustful voice, "You not even going to watch. I know you want some of this."

I never broke my stride to the door nor did I acknowledge her taunts. As I closed the door behind me I stood on the opposite side of the door for a second. I could not help but think about Donald Goines's classic book, Black Girl Lost. I guess too much had not changed since the seventies. This was a modern day black girl lost story. After the courtesy call, I took Tamika home. We drove the whole way in silence until I pulled up in front of her house.

"I guess you're officially on call now!"

She never broke her off in the distance stare. She simply answered, "Yeah, I am on call now!"

"You know Tamika, you don't have to do this if you really don't want to. Twenty-one is relatively young. Learn from other's mistakes. You don't have enough time to make them all yourself."

"Thanks for the philosophy quote but I'm not interested in anything that does not put any money in my pocket." She opened her door and reminded me that she was on call.

# 4
# CHANGING FACES

"True change begins in your heart,
then in your mind and eventually shows in your life."

The first phone call of the morning was from Tee. "Czar I'm glad that you got Tamika processed and available to take calls."

"Not a problem Tee, a new fresh face for this big upcoming weekend will be good money for everybody."

"What's her stage name going to be?"

I responded with a chuckle. "What else but little Miss Persistent?"

We both laughed at the unlikelihood of that. "No seriously, Czar?"

"Okay, how do you like Innocence for her?"

"Huh! I can see that all the way. She does have a girl next door innocence thing going for her, don't she?"

"Yeah, she does. But the real question is for how long?"

"Okay, Innocence it is then."

Escorting is definitely a customer service driven business so we get to know our clients really well. It's important to know your clients and their taste in women. A lot of these guys are very specific as to what they want—height, weight, complexion, etc. I had the perfect first client for Tamika to bust her cherry, so to speak. I set the call up for seven o'clock that evening. I called her and explained the procedure of setting up a call. "Hey Tamika, I have a call set up for you later on."

Very nonchalantly, she responded, "That's what's up."

"How it works is like this. I'll call you from the office phone and then we call the client on three-way without him knowing I'm on the line. This way he never has a direct number to you nor you to him. So you never have to worry about a client harassing you as well as keeping you honest as not to be tempted to client steal." "

"Okay, I got it Czar!"

"When we call a client you're just calling to give a physical description of yourself and get accurate directions, nothing else. They already know the fees from their initial call to the office. Never let anyone draw you into quoting a price to them on the phone, you understand?"

"Absolutely!"

"Solicitation is defined as offering a sexual act for a price, so don't do it. Sex for money is against the law except for in part of Nevada."

"Okay Czar, I'm clear about that."

"I'll pick you up about six o'clock. The call is in Alpharetta so we'll need an hour from the West End to get there on time."

Tamika walked out of her house right on time. She jumped into the passenger seat and flashed me a big hello smile.

I greeted her. "I like what you're wearing, really nice!"

"So you said this guy is a regular right?"

"Yeah he'll be piece of cake. Very successful middle-age white guy. He lives in Florida with his family. During the week he's in Atlanta managing his business here. He's a very generous tipper if you play your cards right."

"Sounds like someone I'd like to meet."

"Do you have any questions?"

"No, not right now."

"Off we go then!"

Tamika turned her body to face me and said, "You know you missed out on the best courtesy call you would have ever had right!"

I was certain that she would comment on yesterday's events. Coolie, "Did I? I don't think I missed anything. All I want is this money you're about to give me sweetheart."

"Yeah right, I see how you looked at me. Did you forget I felt blood rush to your dick with minimum effort on my part? What's the deal with you Czar?"

I searched my ashtray for two quarters to pay the fifty cent toll on GA-400. I tossed the coins into the basket and accelerated forward.

"Are you just going to ignore me Czar?"

"What would you like me to say babe?"

"I don't know, but there is certainly something different about you than most men."

I shifted the direction of the conversation. "You have protection?"

"Yes, in my purse."

After driving in silence for a few exits I felt the need to see where this young lady's mind was. "Yo, Tamika, I want you to make this work for you, not the other way around."

"What do you mean?"

"Well I've seen a lot of females start escorting with intentions of just getting a car or an apartment. But they get caught up in the life and before you know it years have passed and they have nothing to show for it."

"Well that's not the case with me. I'm not no stupid bitch who has a pimp and shit like that. Like I told you from the get go, I'm about making money."

"Okay, I hear you Tamika." Looking up to see Exit 11, I steered the SUV off the highway and onto the exit ramp. Pulling up to the client's house I reminded her to check in after getting the money in her hand. She jumped out and started walking towards the front door. I watched as her waist swayed from side to side—nothing but hips and thighs. Yeah, she was sexy as ever! I thought to myself, *These young girls are too grown.*

Tamika checked in just like she was supposed to then called and checked out right on time. I was impressed. I figured I would be even more impressed after I called the client for his feedback about her performance and attitude.

Tamika hopped up into the front seat beaming from ear to ear. "Czar you not going to believe this shit." Wide-eyed and full of excitement, she continued with her rant. "You not going to believe this shit; he tipped me an extra hundred and fifty dollars on top of the regular fee. And I promise you he barely touched me. He was very nice. When I walked in he offered me bottled water then we talked a little. He is a very interesting guy; he didn't come from money either. He built his business from the ground up. I followed him up to the master suite which was ridiculous. His walk-in closet was the size of my bedroom. He sat on the edge of the huge king size bed where I walked over and knelt between his legs. When I unzipped his pants I had to search for his extremely small dick."

Tamika started to giggle. "I did everything to compose myself so I wouldn't laugh or stare. Hold on, hold on, that's not the funny part. I finally find his small-ass dick so I start giving him head—he almost bust like in two minutes. I then take off my shoulder straps to let my dress fall to the floor. I mounted him as to ride him and before I could even get a rhythm going, I see his eyes rolling to the back of his head. He begins to moan and mumble, 'I'm coming, I'm coming.' His body tensed up then spasmed a few times and it was over. It was all so very surreal for me Czar. And that was just the first ten minutes of me being there. We both washed up and spent the rest of the time talking downstairs. He's a very intelligent man. All this time I've been letting these nine and ten inch dick black niggas stretch my coochie out of place and for what? Fucking dinner and conversation. Oh no, that shit ends today. Look at all this money I just made for ten minutes worth of work."

I sat there thinking to myself. This was the street poisoning I'd tried so hard to avoid. Once you got a taste it was almost impossible to ever turn back. I did not pick this client randomly. After two years of patronage I already knew his routine if he liked a girl. It would have just been wrong to send her to Big Dick Greg down in Riverdale for her first call. The nigga doesn't tip and he's going to beat the pussy up for one full hour. Or! On second thought that may have discouraged her altogether. I strongly doubt it though—Tamika had already made up her mind. Once again I was reminded that escorting is not about sex. It's about communication and filling an emotional void.

After getting both my fee and the agency fee I just listened to her tell me of all her plans with all the money she was going to make from here on out. She was going to get herself her own car then move downtown to Atlantic Station and so on and so forth.

With all her chatter and excitement the ride back to the West End seemed very fast. I pulled in front of her place. Before getting out, Tamika reminded me that she would be available all night if necessary. I guess the expression that my face conveyed told her otherwise.

"Look Czar I'm trying to get some money tonight. You know you can make some paper driving me too so don't front."

She had a good point. I smiled and replied, "Aight, see you later."

That night I certainly did make money driving Tamika from call to call, a total of five calls to be exact. The Memorial Day weekend was much how we expected it to be—busy! Tamika had more money than she had ever had at any one time in her whole life. She never complained or seemed bothered in the least. Hoeing was waaaaay too natural for her at twenty-one-years-old, damn!

Over the course of the following weeks I saw both a physical and emotional change in Little Miss Persistent. It was only a matter of time before she hooked up with some of the other girls at the agency. Their nights out partying at the Velvet Room, Esso and all the other hot spots that Atlanta had to offer turned into drunken drug induced blurs. I remember my grandmother used to say, "That night air will age you faster than anything." She was right. Tamika had lost that full, girl-next-door look in her face, for a more slender sunken-in profile. She had visible dark patches under her eyes which were now always glazed over. It appeared to me that she was obviously not eating properly at all.

More apparent than her diminishing looks was her overall disposition. Her articulate sweet voice gave way for a more raspy tone. She seemed to have taken on the persona of her new acquaintances, the more seasoned veteran whores. Every word out her mouth was four letters or prepositioned with a bitch or muthafucker. It hurt my ears to hear her talk.

The rumors about Tamika started getting back to me. I subtly questioned other girls she would work with, about her behavior. It was common knowledge that Tamika was sniffing powder cocaine and popping ecstasy pills on a regular basis. Was I the only one in the dark? I felt like a real naive parent for the first time in my life, kind of like, "Oh, not my child!" I'd been in the streets all of my life. How did I not see this? I knew she was doing a lot of partying. I thought the change in her face and behaviors was a result of too much drinking and weed smoking at worst. But to think that after just two months of working at the agency, she was doing hardcore drugs was not conceivable to me. Had I been out of touch with the street life that long? From what I was told, Tamika had been introduced to and offered drugs by a few different clients who liked to indulge while enjoying a pretty young girl. I was fully aware of clients partaking in their own vices. But I was sure I went over that in the orientation with her. I told her clients were going to offer her drugs and to just say no. Stupid bitch! I was way too emotionally invested in this one. I had to step back and be objective. Clients were not complaining and she was still making the agency a ton of money. I was out of the Captain Save-a-Hoe business anyway. I foresaw this from the start and I did not want to be right. I'd give her a few weeks, a few months at best, before she got herself into some real deep shit. I could guarantee that!

When someone is using drugs or alcohol they lose their ability to reason and make good decisions. I could never understand addictions. I had excessive compulsive behaviors so it was clear to me not to drink or do any drug. Coupled with my father's past heavy drinking, I was certainly predisposed to alcoholism. Doing drugs and smoking weren't options for me either. I never crumbled to peer-pressure, taking the perspective that everything I'm not, makes me everything I am.

I didn't think Tamika succumbed to any type of peer pressure though. I was certain she was using drugs and alcohol as an escape. It was like I had an epiphany. I'd been doing this long enough to pick up on personalities. From day one, I noticed that she took to hoeing way too naturally. Now it was clear that she was using drugs as a clutch to help cope. I wanted to treat Tamika like any other hoe that had come through the agency but my spirit just would not let me. I would have to address her sooner or later.

Could I be a one man intervention? Could an intervention consist of just one person? I formulated a plan, to call Tamika, set up lunch with her and then somehow have her and Beverly become acquainted with each other. Beverly was so different than all the girls that I'd ever seen come through the agency. I knew she would be a positive influence on Tamika. Beverly was a consistent 4.0 student at Spelman. The cliché of a girl becoming an exotic dancer or escort to pay her way through school was actually true in her case. Beverly was truly focused on school and building a future to separate herself from this business. She was in the sex business but not of it if you know what I mean. While so many other girls spent their money on Gucci, Coach and Louis Vuitton bags as well as tattoos, clothes and partying, she kept a very modest lifestyle. Yeah, Beverly would certainly help me out with putting Tamika back on track.

I read somewhere that it's best to have hard conversations in a public setting. I guess this way the exchange couldn't really get too heated if it was held somewhere like at a restaurant table. My plan was to invite Tamika out to lunch. Thai food was one of my favorites. I particularly liked Top Spice which has the best coconut shrimp soup ever. I started warming up to the idea of talking with Tamika more and more. I wouldn't approach it like a task but more like a concerned big brother.

There was no point in me procrastinating so I dialed Tamika's number right then and there. The phone rang twice before she picked up.

"Hey Czar what's up, you got a call for me?"

"Nah, I was just giving you a call to see how things have been going for you. We have not really had a chance to talk outside of you taking calls."

"Uh oh, not Czar making a social phone call," Tamika teased. "Let me find out you sweet on Mika Mik."

"You real funny Tamika, I'm not sweet on Mika Mik at all." Laughing I added, "I start hitting that then you think you don't have to take calls and make the agency money anymore huh!"

We both had a good laugh before I suggested that I come pick her up for lunch. We agreed on one-thirty for me to pick up at her place. I could not gather anything outside of the norm from our chat. It's one thing to sit across from someone and look them in their eyes, and another to communicate over the phone.

The next step in my plan was to contact Beverly and subtly suggest that she take Tamika under her wing. I knew going in that this would pose more of a challenge. Beverly did not think the other girls were on her level; not in a snobbish, "I'm better than they are" way, but more of an, "I'm not proud of what I'm doing, let me not assimilate with the industry" type of way. Beverly had seen just about the same amount of bullshit that I'd experienced so she kept on blinders. I knew for a fact that Beverly would be in class so I sent her a simple text that read, "Give me a call. I need a very small favor." Most girls at the agency understood the Favor System. Some girls understood it too well for their own good. I'd been in situations where they have wanted to force favors upon me for preferential treatment, if you know what I mean!

I had always found it to be so insulting any time a woman tried to manipulate me with sex. That might be the quickest way to get on the bottom of the call list. Now those on top of the call list got there by simply doing what they were supposed to do which was taking care of the clients with no issues.

After my phone call to Tamika and text to Beverly, I needed to start getting myself together because it was already about 12:15 P.M.

I pulled up in front of Tamika's house at 1:20 P.M., blew the horn once and she walked out at 1:22 P.M. One thing about this business, it will teach you punctuality. The biggest complaints we heard from clients were about girls showing up late. A lot of these executives were stealing an hour here or doing a late lunch there, so time was imperative to them. I also found that consistent punctuality was the easiest way to lure clients who had been loyal to other agencies over to us. The girls knew that not being ready and on time would affect their bottom line. Besides the twenty dollar late fee the agency imposed, they knew that a driver would not put up with their pattern of not being ready because that would mess the driver's money up as well. So, typically after the first week of fines and missing calls, the average girl would get it real fast. So, in an around-about way, you could say I was teaching these girls job readiness skills—time management!

Tamika jumped into the front seat and mumbled, "Hey," under her breath.

"What's good Mama," I answered as I attempted to subtly scrutinize her.

She must have caught the vibe as she stared back at me. "What's wrong with you? WHY ARE YOU LOOKING AT ME LIKE THAT?" She was obviously irritated before even entering the car. Drug users are seldom pleasant to be around without drugs in their systems.

The look I shot at her must have spoken volumes. Tamika apologized for snapping at me without a word being uttered. This was about to go from a nice, tactful intervention to a more volatile one, real fast. I jumped on I-20 East from the West End, merged on to I-85/75 North and exited on North Druid Hills. We drove straight for another four miles until we turned right, into the Toco Hills Plaza where Top Spice was located. We had a bunch of small talk on the way. Tamika could not sit still in her seat; she did a lot of fidgeting. She also had a few very vague phone calls when she got into the car. You know the types with responses like, "Yes… not really… okay… I'll call you back." Outside of that, she was pretty much expressionless, not her usual chatty self.

This was not going to be a long lunch; I had made up my mind to cut to the chase and straight out address her. Whether or not she would come clean and be totally honest was another story. We entered the restaurant and were ushered to a corner booth. The atmosphere was dim and very serene; there was a Zen type feel in the air. The restaurant had very few people dining in. we had missed the lunch crows seeing that it was already like two o'clock by the time we were seated. The waitress placed two glasses of ice water in front of both of us and asked if we needed a moment before we decided what we'll order. I told her give us five minutes to look over the menu, she smiled and walked away. I looked across the table from me to see Tamika holding her head down.

"Hey, Tamika."

Tamika snapped to attention as if she was in a daze.

"Tamika, we need to talk."

"Look Czar, I already know what this whole lunch thing is about."

"Okay, tell me then. No need to prolong it right?"

"All these hoes do is run their mouths. I'm the new bitch on the scene making a bunch of money so they want to hate on me. What I do on my time is my fucking business."

"Well, that's the thing, you're getting high with clients so that makes it my business. There are only a few reasons the police department fucks with escort agencies. One is if they suspect that we have anyone who is not of legal age—minors! Two is if they suspect that we are robbing our clients whether strong arm or credit card thief. And the third reason the police would come knocking is if they suspect we are in anyway involved with the trafficking of drugs. Listen, I'm not going to lose my business for your junkie-ass."

"Junkie!" Tamika repeated the word as if it was a trigger. "You act like I smoke crack. I sniff a little powder occasionally to cope with this bullshit I'm doing to my body and myself." Tamika was more than just visibly shaken up. Tears were streaming down her face at this point. I could see the waitress heading in our direction. I handed Tamika her glass of water and napkins to compose herself.

"Are you guys ready to order?"

I spoke up first knowing that Tamika had not even opened the menu. I ordered for both of us. "Yes, the young lady will have the mild chicken fried rice and I'll have the spicy shrimp fried rice with an extra order of cucumbers on the side."

The waitress avoided eye contact with Tamika. Tears always seem to make strangers uncomfortable.

"Will that be it?"

"No, add two Thai teas as well, thank you."

The waitress briskly walked away with the order slip in hand.

I looked back to Tamika and as if my gaze said to continue, she commenced to share the story of her harsh upbringing in different homes which included the experience of being molested over and over. The tears openly flowed prompting me to move and sit directly by her side. I placed my arms around her shoulders and pulled her close to me. Whatever she was muttering was inaudible to me but I knew it was expressions of hurts of years gone by. She had obviously been holding on to it and just needed to let it out.

We sat in silence for a while with my arms around her until the sniffling stopped. She got up and walked to the restroom. I sat there asking myself how this became my problem? Oh I remembered. I was on some Captain Save-a-Hoe shit. If I was a pimp I would probably have gone down in history as being the worst pimp ever. I did not have the heart for that. Or, maybe I had too much heart to do that. I once worked with a pimp by the name of Rap. He had a burgundy Bonneville. He used to keep two hoes in the trunk of his car if they were *bad*. I bullshit you not. He would pull up on Stewart Avenue, pop the trunk and two bitches would jump out. Cold-blooded man, cold-blooded. Yeah, Tamika was not the only one that was searching for a change. I had to reexamine my own choices as well.

Tamika returned from the restroom more composed and poised. She apologized for her breakdown. "Did I embarrass you?"

"Not at all Tamika, I don't care about these people in here." I hushed her as they brought our food to the table.

"Mmm, looks good thank you."

"Is there anything else I can bring for you?"

"No, thanks we're all set here."

"Well, enjoy."

I think I guarded my profession more than the hoes did. Tamika began to talk again as the waitress departed. "Czar I don't know why you're taking an interest in me but I've never had anyone look out for me without wanting something in return. I just have not figured out what that something is with you. I never thought in a million years that I would try cocaine. After the first time, it just made functioning and taking calls so much easier. At first I just could not see beyond making money. Now, I've saved more money than I've ever had in any one point in my life. But I can't even look at myself in the mirror. A matter of fact, I don't even recognize who I am anymore. You have no idea what it's like to have four to six different men penetrate your body and touch you every day. And I have to put on a smile and act like I'm enjoying it."

Tamika was speaking in a low deliberate tone as she continued. "I speak to some of the girls when we go out. And I found out that Princess has been doing this for ten years. I asked her age and she said she was twenty-six. That means she's been selling pussy since she was sixteen years old. The thought of that was so scary to me Czar. Is that my same fate? I don't want to become Princess. I've changed so much in such a short amount of time. I feel trapped without a whole lot of options."

At that moment my phone alerted me of an incoming text message. "Excuse me for a minute."

While she ate, Tamika gestured with her fork and a nod that I could take it.

It was Beverly returning my text. "Not a problem Czar, I'd love to help in any way that I can. Just give me a call later."

After reading the text I looked up at Tamika and said, "We already have some options. Let me explain it to you like this. True change begins in your heart, then in your mind and eventually it will show in your life."

Tamika nodded her head in agreement and said, "I really receive those words Czar. I sincerely feel you on that one."

Looking up from my own plate, I said, "We just need to come up with a plan for you to make that transition. I have someone I want you to meet. Her name is Beverly. She's a Spelman student and both of you have a lot in common. I know she's going to be a positive influence in helping you make changes in your life."

"As long as she ain't no stuck up chick, I'd love to meet her Czar."

"Not at all, Beverly is very down to earth. Tamika, change is not going to come easy. If the intent is there with action you'll get where you want to go. Just be clear on where you want to go."

"Damn Czar, I love the way you make things sound. You have such a way with words, so poetic when they come off your lips. Maybe you should be a writer or something."

"Thanks! Maybe one day I will be a writer; tell your life story, *From the Hood to Doing Good*." We both laughed at the corny title. "How do you like what I ordered for you?"

"Oh, I'm loving it. Can't you tell? My plate is almost clean."

"I actually do write a little, so give me your email address before we leave and I'll share some of my poetry with you."

She smiled and scribbled her email address down on the corner of piece of paper before tearing the edge off and handing it to me. "I can't wait to read some of your stuff."

The sullen, depressed young lady that walked into the restaurant was long gone. I think I offered her hope, which was more valuable than a lot of things. Tamika had questioned my motives and what I was getting from helping her. What she did not know was that I was experiencing my own personal growth as to my own involvement in the sex industry. Even though I never forced, coerced nor manipulated any females to work for the agency, I was still perpetuating the demise of many young women. I had learned to be so detached from each of those girls over the years. But there was something about Tamika's spirit that would not allow me to exploit her in that way, even if she was willing to exploit herself. I always remembered the rule of street poisoning—once you get a taste, it's a wrap. Whether she knew it or not, Tamika was helping me as much as I was helping her.

I wondered what Tee would think if she knew I was out here reforming hoes. The thought made me laugh to myself. She certainly did not give a fuck about any of these chicks. My aspirations were so much bigger than this agency so it was not hard for me to walk away, if need be. Tamika did not even know of my desire to write, so it was such a compliment for her to clearly see it in me, without any previous notion.

As I sat across from Tamika, I just stared at her while she went on and on about something, being her old chatty self. It was like I could not hear a word she was saying because I was really caught up in how the life came back into her spirit. It was all in slow motion, the grand hand gestures she was making, the sparkle that was back in her eyes. Tamika was so bright, as were a lot of these girls. They really could do anything they wanted to set their minds to. They opted to do what seemed like the easier way when in actuality it was the harder way. Princess could have earned a master's degree in just about any field she wanted but instead she had invested ten years on her back with her legs open. I realized that growing up in the 'hood, we tend to deal with the immediate needs—clothing, food and shelter. These girls were so resilient and ambitious that they could be running successful businesses of their own. It reminded me of most of their male counterparts who chose the hustle game. Some of our brightest young men were sitting in jail cells around the country because it made more sense to them to make five thousand dollars a week, versus five hundred dollars a week. Both these young men and these young women had the right aim, just the wrong target.

"Did you hear anything I said? Czar, did you?" I snapped out of my day dream to Tamika's voice. "Czar are you listening to me?"

"Yeah babe, go on!"

"Lunch was great. You ready to go?"

"Yeah, I'm ready babe." I motioned the waitress to bring the check. I paid the bill and we headed out the door. Outside, our eyes had to readjust from being in the dimly lit restaurant to now being in the sun. Tamika grabbed my arm as we walked to the SUV. I hoped she didn't think that this was a lunch date. Either way, I did not pull away. It actually felt pretty good. We stopped in front of the truck and she embraced me tightly. She closed it out with a soft kiss on the cheek. "Thank you Czar. I really needed that."

"No problem babe!" I came around and opened the passenger door for her. Tamika paused and looked me deeply in my eyes before hopping in. Hadn't a man opened a car door for her before? Her gaze followed me through the front windshield window to the driver's side door. She then reached over and popped my door for me. The effort to return the favor did not go unnoticed, as I thanked her. Back on the highway we headed south on I-85. I looked over to my right only to see Tamika beaming back at me with a goofy smile.

"What's up babe?"

"Czar, you know what's up! You not feeling me or you just can't fuck with a hoe?"

Huh! I did not know how to respond to that. There was an awkward silence in the car until Tamika spoke again.

"Well, Chocolate Boy Wonder?" She hesitated for a moment. "Well, isn't that the name a few girls at the agency gave you?" I was visibly blushing as dark as I am. "You don't have to answer now Czar I'm patient. I already told you how these hoes talk. And let me tell you, I like what I'm hearing." Tamika was being so seductive and flirtatious, she started touching her breast. I did everything mentally I could to stop the blood from rushing to my groin area. I focused on the road with my eyes straight ahead, holding the steering wheel textbook style, at ten and two o'clock. One thing I learned in this business was which head I needed to think with. I also did not want to destroy the chance of a future trice with Tamika. So, I had to handle this delicately, leaving the door open for a future opportunity.

"Tamika, I find you very attractive, believe me but there is a place and time for everything."

From Tamika's expression I could tell that my reply satisfied both her ego and the suggestion that something could pop off between us in the future. I learned the hard way, a long time ago, that women don't handle rejection well. Trust me on that.

Tamika was relaxed in her seat now. "Don't forget to have your friend Beverly give me a call. I'm looking forward to opening up my circle to people who could feed into my life."

"I'm going to give her a call as soon as I drop you off."

"I really enjoyed our time together today."

"I did as well Tamika."

"When I get home I'm going to seriously begin thinking of what I want to do with my life."

"No time like the present babe, get right on it."

As we drove through the city, I thought about what a beautiful sunny day it was. I pulled up to Tamika's house. She exited and made her way over to the driver's side window. "Don't forget to email me some of your poetry."

"I certainly will babe." After I answered her, she just kind of stood there. It was an awkward and very long twenty seconds of just looking at each other. I put the car in drive and kind of just slowly pulled away.

I dialed Beverly's number as soon as I left Tamika's, just as I had promised.

Beverly picked up right away. "What's up Czar!"

"Just chillin', you know how it is. What about you?"

"Well, school is keeping me more than enough busy. I'm taking a call here and there but I'm really excited about graduating this year."

"I'm excited for you as well."

"You know you have to come to my graduation."

"I won't miss it for anything Mama."

"Good! What is it that you wanted to talk to me about Czar?"

"Well, Beverly, I've taken on a project that will need more of a woman's delicate touch and finesse. I thought to myself if anyone can pull it off it's going to be Beverly."

Now laughing, Beverly responded. "Look Czar you don't have to butter me up. What is it?"

"Well, I have a new hire that needs some direction. She's a really sweet girl who just hasn't had a break in life. I have enough wisdom and experience to tell you how this story ends if we don't intervene now."

"Let me understand this correctly, you want me to babysit a grown-ass woman?"

"C'mon Beverly, not babysit. Just share some of the things you're doing with your life."

"You know I don't socialize with the girls from the agency."

"I know, I know. You know I wouldn't ask if I really wasn't digging her."

"You must be hitting it Czar."

"Nah, I swear to you I have not laid a hand on her. How many times have I come through for you Beverly? Who was there for you when your ex was whipping that ass? That was no walk in the park. That Decatur nigga did not have it all."

"I know Czar."

"How about that time you were stranded in Miami?"

"Why you got to bring that up, huh!" I could visualize Beverly's big grin through the phone. At this point I knew she was going to help me out. "I don't believe you went there with the Miami story! We said we were not going to bring that up ever again. I need you to promise."

"Cool, you do this and it's forgotten forever."

"Okay Czar, we have a deal."

# 5

# BEVERLY

"Intuitions are glimpses of faint
residue captures of your past life."

rowing up in the suburbs of Chicago, Beverly had a
fairytale upbringing. She was the only child of two
loving parents who had been high school sweethearts.
Her father had come from very humble beginnings rooted in the
south. He later earned a business degree and opened up his own
used car lot. He did well for himself and his family; well enough
to move the family into the Bolingbrook community.
Bolingbrook was thirty minutes outside of Chicago. Beverly had
attended private schools as long as she could remember.

Beverly was also the epitome of *daddy's little girl.* Her father
loved her more than anything in the world. He spoiled her with
lavish birthday parties and extreme gifts on holidays. Beverly's
dad knew she deserved every bit of it; she had always been a
good child and an A+ student. Beverly started to read and do
complex math very early on in life. Even though Beverly's mom
had earned a degree in sociology, she opted not to work and be
a housewife and homemaker. Outside of taking care of both the
home and Beverly, she was a social staple in the community.

Volunteering for this or always organizing that, she was the social butterfly of Bolingbrook, Illinois.

Spending summers in Massachusetts in Martha Vineyard's Oak Bluff area, surrounded by colorful gingerbread Victorian homes, was commonplace for the family. They forged relationships with other well-to-do blacks at the popular Ink Well beach. By the time Beverly was fourteen years old she had traveled throughout most of the Caribbean—Trinidad and Tobago, St. Thomas Virgin Islands, Jamaica and the Bahamas. She matured very early from the exposure to the world she had as a young girl. Even though she was an only child and spoiled, Beverly had developed a keen sense of resilience and self-reliance. Despite her parents' protests, Beverly got her working papers at sixteen and went right to work at a fast food restaurant. Her parents could not make heads or tails of why their daughter would want to go to work in a fast food restaurant, but they eventually came around and supported her. That was typical Beverly for you—she wanted to make her own way.

Beverly graduated at the top of her class from high school. Her parents were elated that she received acceptance letters from UCLA and Stanford, as well as Notre Dame, her father's Alma mater. However, in typical Beverly form, she opted to attend a historically black college or university, an HBCU. She finally decided on Spelman College in the heart of Atlanta as opposed to Howard University in the nation's capital. When Beverly and her mother visited Howard's open house, the frigid weather and the city's reputation for crime lost out to the blistering summers and the thriving black population of Atlanta, Georgia. This would be the first time Beverly would live apart from her parents. While it was nerve-wrecking for her parents to think about their baby girl being several states away on her own,

Beverly could not wait to embrace her newfound independence. In the fall, the family packed up the SUV and took the trek to Atlanta. Since it was mandatory that first-year Spelman students live on campus, she settled into her room in the LLCI dormitory.

Beverly's first year at Spelman was no surprise to anyone. She made friends easily and excelled in all of her classes. She was dating like any typical college girl her age—no one serious though. Beverly fell in love with the city almost immediately, spending countless hours at the High Museums on Peachtree Street or The Fernbank Museum of Natural History off of Ponce de Leon Avenue. Beverly truly appreciated the arts. By her second year she was well acquainted with Atlanta. There was not a landmark in the city that she had not been to at least twice. The Aquarium was one of her favorite places to spend time alone, not to be outdone by the zoo or the beautiful Botanical Garden.

Beverly would spend summers back in the Chi' with her mother and father. They would use this time to vacation together and reconnect. Beverly's dad could see his daughter blossoming right in front of his eyes. He dreaded the sex talk with his baby girl. Little did he know, she had been experimenting down in Atlanta for more than a year now. Her father had no idea how to approach the subject as was typical of many fathers.

So, he simply asked, "Are you dating?"

Beverly was a little startled by the out of left field question. She turned to him and took his hand and said, "Yes dad and I am being safe in all that I do."

With that, they embraced. Beverly felt the warm comfort of her father's arms but she could not see the one solitaire teardrop that was running down his creek. That which was understood did not have to be said. Beverly loved both her parents very much but at the end of the day she was, daddy's girl.

That summer they vacationed in Hawaii for the very first time. Beverly watched her mom and dad walk hand-in-hand as if it was their first date. Looking on in adoration, hoping to one day find a love like that brought tears to her eyes. As she watched them along the seashore, she asked herself what she would ever do without her daddy. Beverly experienced a great sense of growth that summer. The family returned to Chicago and Beverly returned to school for her third year. At this time she was no longer living on campus with the first and second year students. She found a nice gated apartment complex in Midtown that was a great fit for her needs. She decided to take a job in a retail store in Perimeter Mall. Between work and school Beverly stayed occupied.

It was in the second semester of her third year that tragedy would strike the family in a way that was so unexpected. Beverly's dad left his business on the way to the bank to make a deposit. While in his car, sitting at a red light, he was bumped from behind. When he got out to inspect the car, he was met by two men, one brandishing a gun.

The one with the gun said, "Give me that muthafucking deposit bag."

The other man said, "We've been watching you for two weeks now. We know what you got."

Before Beverly's father could comply, there were two shots fired—one, hitting him square in the chest and the second hitting him in his head.

The second robber flinched at the consecutive shots. The muzzle flash and roar sent him into a panic. He was certainly shocked by the actions of his partner. "You didn't have to shoot him!" He ran over to the now bloody body to retrieve the deposit bag which they knew he tucked into his waistband.

Beverly's dad's hand gripped the blood-drenched bag tightly, as it was pried away from him. With his last breath he faintly sounded the name "Bev…er…ly…!"

The deposit totaled less than five thousand dollars, which he would have happily handed over. No one would ever know why or what made the gunman fire. The fact was that Beverly's dad now laid dead.

That unfortunate day of Beverly's dad's murder was anything but typical for her. She woke up ready to go to school but was overwhelmed with nausea. Beverly looked at the calendar and knew that she was nowhere near her cycle. The knots in her stomach puzzled her. She thought it might have been something she ate. She certainly knew that she was not pregnant. Despite her initial thoughts to stay home, Beverly dragged through the school day. Every class was a laboring experience, each one harder than the last. Although she completed the school day, she just could not muster up the strength to go to work. After making the call to her manager, informing her that she would not be in to work (which was met with indifference to say the least), Beverly went home and was overtaken with unexplained melancholy. The pit of her stomach was entangled with knots and she had lost her appetite since earlier in the day. Her only resolve was to get in the bed and sleep through this hoping that it would pass. Beverly tossed and turned for about forty minutes before falling into a deep, comforting sleep. That evening Beverly dreamed about her childhood growing up with such loving parents. She dreamed more of her daddy whom spoiled her with all of her hearts desires. It was just yesterday that he had called and asked if his little princess was doing well and if there was anything that he could do. She told him no she was doing fine and couldn't wait to see him and her mother. They had exchanged, "I love you's," and hung up the phone.

Three hours later and still deep into sleep, Beverly was awakened by the ringtone of her phone. Reaching for the phone in the now darkened room with her right hand and rubbing her eyes with her left, she realized that she had missed more than a dozen calls from the number simply titled, *HOME.*

Beverly pressed the answer button on her phone and held it up to her ear. All of a sudden, it was as if the earth had stopped on its axis. Everything went into slow motion mode. The hysterical voice on the other line was not making any sense at all. It was barely comprehendible but was obviously her mother.

"Mom, mom, stop crying! What did you say? I could not make out what you were saying!"

"YOUR FATHER WAS MURDERED TODAY BEVERLY! THEY MURDERED MY HUSBAND!"

This was not making any sense to Beverly. Who? What? No, it must be some mistake.

The words were driven home to Beverly the second time around. "Beverly, your daddy was shot dead in the street today!"

Her mother could not console herself. It was a mixture of tears and sobbing that delivered the venomous words.

"No mom, I just spoke to him yesterday. He's okay."

Upon hearing the words yet a third time, denial quickly gave way to a deep, piercing wailing from the bowels of Beverly's spirit. "BEVERLY, YOUR FATHER IS DEAD BABY."

Beverly dropped the phone to the floor and her helpless body followed soon after. She laid there curled up in a fetal position with the phone lying a foot from her head. She could hear and feel her mother's pain through the phone. It was second to her own pain that she was feeling. She could hear the sound of her mother's voice calling to her in vain from on the phone. "Beverly, Beverly! Beverly, are you there sweetheart?!"

Beverly had gone totally mute; she could not answer even if she tried. She laid there on that floor for what seemed like hours. Her body involuntarily shook and quivered. Tears from her sorrows had soaked the tee shirt that she was wearing. Laying there on the floor, hands clasped between her knees that were curled to her chest, she was that infant child again. Beverly unknowingly cried herself back to sleep right there on the floor of her apartment.

When Beverly awoke the following morning, she seemed very shocked at the fact that she was laying on the floor. She thought it was all part of a bad dream. The dried-up tears confirmed that it was very much real and not a dream at all. Beverly started to compose herself as best as she could. Looking at her phone, she had missed several calls and voice messages. No doubt, it was friends and family offering their condolences, trying to console her. Beverly was not in the state of mind to hold a conversation with anyone. It all made sense to her now, the morning nausea and loss of appetite. She was emotionally connected to her father on so many levels. His spirit was certainly trying to warn his little girl. Intuitively she knew something was wrong but what? They say intuitions are glimpses of faint residue captures of your past life. Beverly got up and took a warm soothing bath. After getting out of the bath she put on a comfortable sweatsuit and braced herself for the phone call that she so dreaded. By the time Beverly called her mother they both were over the initial shock of her father's murder.

"Hey mom, are you okay?"

"I'm fine baby. I was more worried about you. Your dad was a very special, special husband and father."

"I know Mom." She felt herself getting emotional again so she shifted the conversation to the business at hand. "Moms, I'm going to book a flight for later today."

"I can't wait to hug you." Beverly could hear the tearful words through the phone and did not want to chime in with her own tears, so she quickly wrapped up their conversation before her voice could start cracking. She hung up the phone and it dawned on her, *My father is dead!*

The next few weeks were more of a haze than any other time in Beverly's life. The trip out to Chicago. The actual funeral. The family she had not seen in years. She did not stay any longer then she needed to. The house just had too many telltale reminders of her father. The time in Chicago was an emotional roller coaster to say the least. There were moments of laughter with family and friends while they reminisced on her dad's whacky humor, then teary-eyed flashbacks of his sensitivity towards both Beverly and her mother.

Upon arriving back to Atlanta, Beverly tried her best to fall back into the routine of work and school. To say it was a challenge would be grossly understating the effort it took each day to act as if the passing of her father did not affect her. The job was not sensitive to the time off that was necessary for Beverly to attend her father's burial. They needed to have a body there so they simply replaced her.

After several months of her mother footing her tuition, rent and several other bills, Beverly decided to get back out and earn her own keep. Her mother still was not working herself nor was she ready to get back out into the workforce. After all, she had been a housewife and homemaker for most of her life. What would she go into at this stage in her life? Beverly understood she was still in mourning for the only man she had ever known or loved. After paying off the debts of the business and creditors, the remainder of the life insurance policy that her father left would be able to carry her mother for only a year or so. If you knew anything about Beverly, she certainly did not want to be a burden on her mother financially. She would get through this last year of school on her own!

The current state of the economy did not help matters much in terms of finding work. Beverly had scaled down her job search expectations tremendously. The simple fact was that no one was hiring. The unemployment rate in Georgia was ten percent. Even worse, that's what the economists were reporting so the actual figures were probably more like twelve to fifteen percent unemployment. Beverly was still not going to be deterred by those reports.

Beverly woke up this particular morning, looked herself in the mirror and made an affirmation: "I will not come back to this apartment without a job today."

With that said, a peace came over her as if it was already done. She took out her smartest-looking business suit and headed out to Lenox Mall. She knew that her smart and sexy look was bound to land her employment today, at the very least, get her in the door. Her hair and nails were impeccable and her heels were high but not whorish. She was very confident four applications and short screenings later although she could never tell after leaving an interview since all parties had a poker face on. You know the scenario—a lot of smiling and handshakes accompanied by, "We'll notify you either way. Thank you." Unfortunately, way too many times before, notification had come on a postcard in the mail regretfully letting Beverly know that another candidate had been chosen for the position.

Beverly was confident that she had made an authentic effort to find a job so she decided to take a leisurely stroll through the mall. The walk in the mall was anything but uneventful. Well-dressed men approached her at every turn. White men, Black men and even an Asian gentleman, commented on how "sexy her shoes made her legs look."

Stopping in front of the Louis Vuitton store to admire the new collection, she was astonished at the price tag on some of the purses. She wanted to go in but what would be the point? As she stood there contemplating her next move, out walked two girls no older than she was with Louis Vuitton shopping bags in both hands. The taller of the two, a shapely caramel-complexioned, chinky-eyed girl with questionable double-D tits walked directly up to her and said, "You don't have to be a window shopper as pretty as you are."

The tall girl's directness and accent told Beverly she was definitely a New Yorker.

"I don't think I would ever want to spend that much on a pocketbook."

"Girl please! If you're getting it, why not spend it," the girl responded. With that said, she looked at her shorter companion and slapped her a high-five. Both ladies were laughing as if there was a punchline that they alone knew.

Ms. New Yorker stood way too close to Beverly as she introduced herself. "My name is Princess and this is my homegirl Cherry."

The shorter one, now known as Cherry, flashed an artificial smile. "Hi."

Beverly introduced herself. After all, she was a bit intrigued with these two girls. "I'm Beverly."

With Princess less than six inches from Beverly's face, Beverly could tell that Princess was into women as well as men. Princess's deliberate delivery and New York accent made people listen to her that much more intensely. "Look Bitch, you are too muthafucking fine to be out here embarrassing yourself window shopping."

Beverly could tell that the words easily sailed out of her mouth; this was obviously not the first time she had had such a conversation. Cherry was shaking her head in agreement—was it a conversation she had heard at some point?

Princess went on, saying, "Look, take this," as she reached inside of her purse and pulled out a sterling silver business card holder. She handed Beverly a gold business card with black writing that simply said *Escort* and a phone number. "Look, call that number and ask for Czar!"

"Who?"

"Czar, like Julius Caesar but just Czar!" Princess picked back up the Louis Vuitton bags she had temporarily put down and looked Beverly deeply in her eyes. She continued, "You know what it is." With that she walked away, Cherry in tow. Beverly certainly did know *what it was*.

Beverly's chance meeting with Princess preoccupied her mind for the rest of the day. She had no idea that that chance meeting would change her life.

The next morning, Beverly woke up and reminded herself of her previous morning's affirmation. After having breakfast and a refreshing shower she got dressed. She grabbed her purse which had the gold business card in it and dialed the ten digits on it. "Hello, can I speak to Czar."

Let's just say the rest is history. Beverly was officially on call after that fateful day. That's how she and I met. From the initial phone conversation, I knew Beverly was not like the typical girls that sought work from me. Meeting her in person later that day galvanized it.

# 6
# ILL OF THE GAME

"The grass is always greener
on the other side until you get the water bill."

Outside of running the agency, I seemed to have turned into a fucking social worker. Not only was it taking away from what I needed to get done, I now had gotten Beverly deputized as my social worker assistant. Sometimes I asked myself why I didn't just get a regular nine-to-five like everybody else? That thought usually lasted all of five seconds while I laughed to myself. This shit is hard work. I manage anywhere between twenty-five to thirty different personalities on almost a daily basis. Some men don't or can't put up with even one bundle of emotions, also known as *woman*.

Beverly had initiated contact with Tamika and they seemed to hit it off quite well over the phone. They had set up a lunch date to do a face-to-face meet later in the week. With Beverly helping with my Save-a-Hoe project, I could now shift my attention to the business at hand.

Running the agency was a clandestine operation and it was never a good idea in my mind's eyes to just openly tell anyone and everyone what I did for a living. The few people who did know always seemed intrigued and the first question would inevitably be, "How did you get into the business?"

My answer was always the same. "I like money and fine freaky-ass women." It was just natural to put them together. I would typically get a laugh out of my response but it was the God-honest truth. The reality of it all could not really live up to the hyped-up fallacies. Maintaining a successful agency was extremely expensive. Full page advertisements easily cost between ten and twelve hundred dollars a month per magazine.

Not only was it very hands-on, very few people saw the bullshit that came with the nature of the business. I had to be on my toes twenty-four/seven. Earlier that day, Victoria, aka Sunshine, had taken a call in a pretty upscale neighborhood in Buckhead. According to her, this muthafucker slipped her a few fake fifty dollar bills. When I got the call, both Malik and Sunshine had just pulled away from the client's house and were now parked on his street. Malik was on the phone running it down to me.

"Yeah, Czar this fucker dropped some play money on us. Could you believe this shit?"

I'd been doing this long enough to know that I had to look at this with a three hundred-sixty-degree eye. Did the client really try to pull a fast one? Or was Sunshine trying to get slick with some paper? "Look Malik, I need you to search Sunshine." Malik immediately perked up and composed himself. "If she followed the rules and left her pocketbook in the car, she should not have any money other than that fee right?"

Malik gave me a subtle, "Uh huh!" while he now looked at his passenger out the corner of his eyes with skepticism and doubt. It never occurred once to Malik that this bitch could be playing him. A pretty face and fat ass can be very disarming.

"Malik, pass the phone to Sunshine I want to talk to her."

Sunshine got on the phone and immediately exploded in my ear, "CZAR, DO YOU BELIEVE THIS BULLSHIT?! THIS MUTHAFUCKER THINK I'M A DUMB HOE OR SOMETHING!"

I listened to her rant for about five minutes straight until I jumped in. "Listen." I raised my voice. "LISTEN! Sunshine if you would have checked the money when he first handed it to you right in front of him, we would not be having this conversation now, would we?"

Reluctantly, her answer came slow. "No, we would not be having this conversation Czar." She then attempted to justify not following the protocol by saying, "Czar, who would have thought with such a nice house and fly-ass cars that he would be on some bullshit."

She was trying to save face and just trying to defuse the situation so I gave her some sympathy. "I know it could have happened to anyone Sunshine." Now came the unpleasant part. I already knew that Sunshine would be offended by me implying that she switched the money herself, but I had a business to run and I needed to be absolutely sure. "Sunshine, I'm going to need you to let Malik search your person."

After a pause she spoke in a very quiet, shaken voice, "Czar, you think I switched the money?"

"I did not say that, but I have to cover all my bases. You could understand that right?"

With a whisper, I heard her answer, "Yeah."

"Give the phone back to Malik." When Malik returned to the phone, I instructed him, "Malik, go ahead and search her."

"Okay Czar, hold on."

I could hear Malik resting the phone down, there was a silence, then a bit of rustling in the background. Malik came back to the phone, "Czar she good!"

I could hear Sunshine whimpering in the background. I could care less about insulting anybody at this point because what came next was no fucking game. "Listen Malik, I'll be over there in fifteen minutes."

I grabbed my jacket and stuck a .40 caliber Glock in the small of my back. I actually made it around there in ten minutes. They were right up the street from the office on Habersham. This was old money Buckhead. What the fuck was this guy trying?

I pulled up next to Malik's car. "Give me the forgazi paper."

He handed it through the window into my awaiting hand. I pulled my truck into the client's driveway and left it running. I knew he was home alone after asking Sunshine a few details. I adjusted the .40 Glock in the back of my waist and walked directly up to the door, ignoring the doorbell and opting for three very assertive knocks. This is where I earned my money. I thought of all the people who asked me why the girls didn't just work for themselves. I thought about the people who questioned the girls' having to pay a driver and an agency when the girls were the ones selling their bodies. I wondered if these same people would have what it took to stand in front of this client door with me. I wondered if they could handle the possible events that could follow.

After some silence, I heard a very annoyed answer, "Who is it?"

"It's the agency."

There was a pause then the door opened. "Yes, how can I help you?" The six-foot-three blonde-haired man easily was at least two hundred eighty-pounds, obviously lifted weights, and was in great physical shape.

Thinking to myself *I hope I don't have to pop this dude in his knee cap or something*, I looked him directly in his eyes and calmly said, "Sunshine just left here and you inadvertently gave her these bills. I'm sure it was a mistake."

As I handed him the bills, he examined them with a quizzical frown on his face. He then looked at me and my cool demeanor then back at the bills. It was hard to read his face. "Hold on one second."

The door closed behind him. I tensed up knowing there was one bullet in the head of my .40 cal and the safety was off. I cuffed the gun with my right hand, not taking it out but being ready for whatever was to come. The door reopened and he had a wad of bills which he pushed in my direction. With a big smile on his face he said, "Sorry about that."

I accepted the money without even looking at it. There was no doubt in my mind that there was not one fake bill in my hand. I nodded with an unspoken understanding between us as he turned his eyes downward in a moment of shame. He obviously had been found out. I took one step back, about-faced and walked to my still idling SUV. This guy knew he did not have a leg to stand on. He had too much to lose. We knew where he lived. He would have done anything to protect the fact that he frequented escort agencies. Now I had to add his name to the *Bad Client List* that circulated throughout the city from agency to agency. Most of the agencies communicated with each other. A guy like this would just turn around and try the same crap with another service. The Bad Client List was very detailed. It would have the person's name, address, telephone number, which agency reported the incident and a description of what took place. In this case, he attempted to pass fake money. The list had a range of offenders and as many different offences. These were the ills of the game.

It was not all fun and games in this line of work. I could remember taking a call in Lithonia to a residential area. I had Princess and Cherry in the car. The call was for Cherry. My intuitions told me from the jump that something was not right. I pulled up to the address and there was the client outside on his porch with his phone in hand—a black male, about mid-twenties, dressed in jeans and a sweat top. He was about five-foot-eleven, one hundred eighty-five-pounds, and wore a baseball cap—not typically the face of our client base.

Now my experience with clients has been like this. If a client sees that you have a driver, he doesn't really want to be seen. He would typically just open the door when the model knocked or rang the bell. This guy was outside and was not in the least bit intimidated that she was not alone. That was not the weird part. The house had a For Sale sign on the front lawn and there was not one light on in the whole house despite it being ten o'clock at night. The whole house was pitch black. While I was still assessing the scene from the front of the house, greed had Cherry reaching for the handle to exit the car.

"Listen, I don't like the looks of this."

"Czar, you worry way too much nigga."

"As soon as you get in there check in and let me know everything is okay."

"Aight, I will Czar."

I went against every instinct that was telling me not to send her in there. I saw the client greet her at the top of the steps. He flashed a smile and had her walk in the door first. The door closed behind them. It would be no exaggeration if I said that was the longest two minutes of my life. After the first minute, I thought to myself that she should have checked in by now. I started calling her phone to get a confirmation. Her phone was now going directly to voice mail. The house was built on a down slope so the street level was actually mid-level to the house. I had to move quickly. I whipped the SUV around to face the house as to focus my high beam lights directly onto the house. By doing this I could see that I had stirred a number of shadowy figures inside the house.

"Princess keep trying her phone," I instructed as I reached down into my compartment to retrieve my gun.

"Same thing Czar, it's still going directly to voicemail. It must be off."

I jumped out of the vehicle and ran up to the door. I quieted myself with my ear to the door. I could hear frantic muffled screams from Cherry. I looked down at my feet. Luckily I had on my Timberlands; they would make kicking in the door that much easier. My first attempt at kicking the door in went in vain. All it did was alert the occupants inside. On my second attempt, I went with much more pressure and commitment. BLAM! The lock gave way and I was inside. I could hear commotion and cries of "C'mon, let's go!" from the basement.

The SUV lights gave me enough sight to see where I needed to go. I was not fucking around with these lil' niggas. I decided to let them know how real it was. I squeezed off three shots in no particular direction. BOOM! BOOM! BOOM! The roar of the .40 caliber echoed even louder than usual in the empty house. There was a still silence that came over the whole scene. It was completely quiet except for a faint sniffling coming from a pile lying on the basement floor. I walked up to see that that pile was Cherry. The basement rear exit was hanging wide open, no doubt the escape route of her assailants. With the gun in my right hand I picked Cherry up with my left. I walked her back up the stairs and out into the car. She was naked from the waist down but I had picked up a sheet that was on the basement floor to drape around her. Outside of a bruise on her cheek and some marks around her neck, Cherry was not hurt. Like I said, it was the longest two minutes of my life and I suspected of Cherry's too. Princess jumped in the back seat to console her as I pulled out of the neighborhood. We drove for ten minutes before anybody said anything.

It was Cherry who broke the silence in between tears. "Czar, thank you so much. They were trying to rape me."

Princess held her close to her bosom which I suspected was not a part of her body that she was unfamiliar with. "I know Mama, I know. You're safe now!"

The warm gun was still on my lap. As soon as I got back to the office I immediately called several other agencies and made them aware of the incident. I then uploaded it onto the Bad Client List.

Less than a few hours later, another agency had reported that they had gotten a call requesting a model in the same area. I later found out that these guys were using foreclosed homes that were abandoned and for sale to lure girls over in order to then rape them. Somewhere along the line someone had dropped the ball by not reporting the first incident to the Bad Client List and making everyone else aware.

It had only been three days since Beverly agreed to speak to Tamika but I was excited that they had made plans to meet in Atlantic Station to share a few drinks over pizza. Beverly told me that her initial phone conversation with Tamika was really cool. She was glad to see she was not a straight ghetto 'hood chick, which was her greatest reservation. So, the ball was in motion now. I could get back to the daily operations of the agency. While Tee handled a lot of the administrative duties, she left much of the hands-on footwork to me. It really bothered me that so many people did not see the hard work that went into running an agency. And to be frank, it was taking a toll on me in more ways than one. I was available for all of the unforeseen events that could and would take place in routine industry life. That meant that I was on standby pretty much twenty-four hours a day to handle whatever would develop whether agency-related or a crisis in one of the girls' lives. Yeah, I started to question the tradeoff. One of the obvious perks, besides the money, was indeed the access to unlimited unbridled taboo sex. None of the models ever told me no despite any of my, how can I say this, exotic requests.

Most men have only held lifelong fantasies in their imaginations but these were some of my daily escapades. I did not know it but my reputation had preceded me among the models. I was initially annoyed with the kiss and tell that was going on behind the scenes in reference to my libido. What are we, in high school! In time, I not only embraced the sex gossip among the models but I realized that it set the stage for the newcomers. The newcomers knew what it was even before meeting me. We had an unspoken understanding.

The adverse side to all this access to unchallenged sex was that my personal life suffered. I had gotten spoiled and used to having sex on my terms, at my will. I did not want to put the time nor effort into courting and getting to know a lady at all. Outside of my misguided views on sex and relationship, it was really hard for me to date a normal "square" chick. I would go for weeks if I could help it, before I even confided in a young lady as to what I did for a living. Then, on the few occasions that I did disclose the fact that I ran an escort service, it was met with ridicule and judgment. I concluded that a square chick is just too insecure to ever understand or be comfortable with her dude around a bunch of attractive, sexually-charged women.

It was extremely difficult for me to maintain any sense of normalcy in regards to building a relationship. Even though I had numerous freaks at my disposal, I still lacked intimacy. Anyone who has ever truly cared for anyone knows the difference between fucking and making love. Making love was way more gratifying than going through the physical motion of having sex, no matter how fine she was. I had not had a passionate kiss in a very long time; I certainly was not about to kiss any of the girls that worked for the service. God knows where their mouths had been. I truly missed the intimacy of walking in Piedmont Park with that special someone you did not mind being seen with in public. Furthermore, I missed being the chivalrous guy I naturally was. It was second nature for me to open a car door for a lady or show up with two dozen roses but I would be sending mixed message if I did that for these hoes. They would not understand that I was doing it strictly because of who I was and that it had absolutely nothing to do with them or how I felt about them. I sincerely enjoyed making a lady feel like a lady but I could not just do this for anybody. I had very few sleepover guests. It was understood that after our trice, they had to leave. On the occasions when I did entertain a sleepover companion, I could not reward her with breakfast in bed. Again, what sort of message would I be sending to her? It dawned on me that intimacy and monogamy were more my things even if I did not want to openly admit it to myself. The realization was a little scary to me. Could it be that I was growing up? I laughed to myself at the hypocrisy of it all. Many men had intimacy and love at home but they'd risk it all for a moment of lust, even though the lust could never be as fulfilling as the love at home. I had to be honest with myself. What woman would be comfortable with me running an escort service? I would be bringing too much, too soon, into a potentially brand new relationship. How would the introduction go? "Hey, my name is Czar. I run an escort service and I'm always around a lot of pussy. Nice to meet you."

That line would not get me far—at least not far with someone worthy of being called my girl. I took the attitude that she'd need to be secure in herself. However, I had to rethink my stance on that—it was about me making her secure with what we had. Not to mention, the forever available slippery slope of available pussy (no pun intended) around me. How would I feel if the shoe was on the other foot? My girl around a bunch of men that she was physically attracted to? Would I give it all up for true love and intimacy? Only time would tell. It was the ying-yang of the universe again; in everything seemingly good there was a drawback and vice versa. I had some serious thinking to do over the next few months. I could not continue on this way. I certainly wanted someone to call my own, to begin building a future with. The ills of this business began to outweigh its benefits. The grass is always greener on the other side until you get the water bill.

Only a week had passed after the attempted rape of Cherry. Things were seemingly back to business as usual. Episodes like that with gun play were far and few between. Every so often a client would get out of hand with his mouth but by the time I showed up at his door with some muscle, the shit got resolved real fast. Well, today's problem was a beast of another kind—the Atlanta Police Department.

Despite the misconception that escorting is illegal, it's not! Why the police department continuously set up stings was beyond me! A lot of girls that were escorting didn't even know that an escorting permit existed. They simply set up ads on Euros, City Vibe, Backpage, Craigslist and numerous other websites without any legal protection for themselves. Getting an escort permit was as simple as going down to the Atlanta Police Department license and permits office, filling out a short application and paying the two hundred and fifty dollar fee. That fee sure beat the hassle of going through the booking process and ending up in jail, paying a bail, and then possibly a lawyer. These girls just jumped into the game without knowing the rules.

Tee was really good about keeping our business license, escort permit and all the back office items intact. So when I got the call from her saying Aliza had been locked up for solicitation downtown at the Marriott, I was more annoyed than upset.

Aliza was a veteran who had worked with the agency for a solid year; she knew the rules well. I told Tee that I would call her back after I made another phone call.

I dialed Princess's number and she answered on the first ring. "What up Czar!"

"Yo, Mama what's good with your special friend?"

"Who you talking about?"

"Your special friend that tips us off about the happening in the city."

"Oh, you talking about Detective Holder from the vice squad."

"Yeah!"

"Well, I haven't heard from him in a few days."

"I bet you hear from him when he wants some pussy though, right?"

"Well, you know how that goes!"

"Okay, check it, Aliza got knocked downtown at the Marriott hotel. I need you to find out about the details of her arrest from detective Holder."

"Okay Czar. I'll call him now and hit you back."

"Cool Mami."

Everything that I had planned for the day had to be put on hold. The most important thing was to get Aliza out of jail.

I immediately called Tee back. "So what else do you know about Aliza's arrest?"

"Well she was charged with solicitation and is being held at the Fulton County Jail."

"Did you call our guy down at the bail bonds office?"

"Yeah, Czar that was the first thing I did. She has a twenty-five hundred dollar bond so he just wants ten percent of that which is two hundred fifty dollars."

"Okay, good Tee!"

"Czar, when I booked Aliza for the call, his ID matched the guest registry and everything."

"You can't blame yourself. You followed the rules."

"Okay, now we know that vice is registering under their real names now, huh!"

"Was any other agencies hit?"

"Yeah, two others agencies got knocked."

"Did you place it on the bad client's message board?"

"Oh yeah, everyone knows about the bust at that hotel."

"All we can do now is wait for her to be processed and I'll go pick her up. How long do you think that will take?"

"Like about two to three hours."

"Okay Tee, I'll hit you back later."

I had done everything that I could do at this point. Now it was just a waiting game. I had safeguarded against this kind of thing so now curiosity was getting the best of me. Why they would arrest her was the question. This was the bullshit that the people who romanticize escorting did not talk about or see. But again, these were the ills of this industry. It was moments like this that reminded me that I wanted out of this business.

I decided to grab something to eat to kill some time and stay in the downtown vicinity. Eatz on Ponce de Leon would be a great option, not to mention their prices were cheap and they had the bomb turkey lasagna. After ordering my food and sitting down, the phone call that I had been anticipating came through. It was Princess.

I answered the phone. "Tell me something good Mami."

"Well, detective Holder got back to me and said that Aliza was being 'uncooperative'"

"What's that!"

"Code word for she wouldn't fuck or suck none of the officers."

"Exactly, you know it."

"So, she had her escorting permit on her and everything but since they found condoms in her bag they're saying that that shows intent on part of her behavior to have sex."

"These fucking cops are some real dirt bags."

"Aliza is a trooper so I feel secure about her loyalty anyway."

"Let me ask you this Princess. You still got a copy of that tape of you and the good detective Holder?"

"I sure do!"

"Okay, keep it in a safe place I have my copy as well. I need you to start taping all of your correspondence with him too. That's going to be our safety net if shit ever hits the fan."

"Okay Czar, I got you. Tell Tee I'm available to take some calls today. I'm off my period now."

"When did your period ever stop you from working?"

"Ah, you got jokes huh, Czar?"

"No, I'm serious. You were the first person I ever heard of talking about using Insteads while on your period."

"Yeah, sometimes I use it, sometimes I just sit it out."

"Okay, I'll tell Tee to put you on the available roster."

After hanging up with Princess I realized that I knew way too much about things that I did not necessarily need to know about. The average woman did not even know that a product like Insteads even existed. It could be found at any drugstore. Insteads afforded a woman the flexibility of living life while on her cycle. With Insteads a woman could partake in activities such as swimming, sports and, in Princess's case, sex, without a MESS!

After eating, taking some phone calls and driving down to the Fulton County Jail, I got the word that Aliza had made bail. I was there when she walked out and jumped into the front seat. "Hey Czar, you know this is some bullshit right!"

"I already know babe."

"I had my escorting permit and everything. He wanted me to have sex with him and agree to cooperate with investigations in the future. I asked him why would I do that, I'm not breaking the law. He then reached into my bag and pulled out a few condoms. He turned to me and said, 'You're under arrest for solicitation.' I was like, 'for what?' I called him all kind of bitch-asses and pussy this and hoe-ass that!" This was the only time I saw Aliza's smile. She was not upset. She was more annoyed and just plain tired of this lifestyle—these crazy hours, dysfunctional relationships and spirit surfing. It all begins to take a toll on you sooner or later.

"Look Aliza, you know our lawyer is going to get this thrown out. This is a misdemeanor. It would never have any legs."

"Czar, do you think I'm stressing this little bullshit charge? Do you remember when I started working with the agency?"

"Yeah I do."

"Well, I thought that I would just catch up with a few bills, buy a car and then stop. Well a year and some months later, I'm doing the same thing. I have not been in a traditional relationship in that long. I run around lying about what I do to everyone because I'm not proud of it. I can't keep giving my body to strangers. I'm emotionally drained and it's something about a jail cell that brings clarity to us all."

"I totally understand Aliza. We all are looking for an out." When I dropped Aliza off I knew she would never return to the agency. She was burned out. She was officially off call.

I really had to step back from this industry sooner or later too. I had to redirect my focus on the things that I sincerely enjoyed. When I was not handling agency business which was rarely ever the case, I would use my spare time to read or write. Reading was a natural joy for me. My love of books evolved from my early love of comics. It was a seamless transition into novels. I could remember reading all of Judy Blume's books, *Tiger Eyes, Wifey, Smart Women*... I could go on and on. It was not until much later on in life when I read Nathan McCall's first book, *Makes Me Wanna Holler,* that a light went on and shined on the fact that I could write too! In every book there is one line that stands out more so than any other line in the book. For me, that line came out of Nathan McCall's book: "If your life was not worth writing about, it was not worth living."

I thought to myself about my early days growing up in Crown Heights, Brooklyn, NYC and then my subsequent years in the streets of Baltimore, Maryland hustling. I certainly had a story to tell. I thought I had way more of a colorful life than Mr. McCall. Writing became escapism for me; it allowed me to express ideas, emotions and opinions freely. I especially found poetry therapeutic. One can take a particular subject matter and quickly pour out feeling with wit, humor, emotions and understanding and move on to the next topic or issue. Yeah, writing helped me to deal with much of the bullshit that came with this industry. It didn't matter how many different situations or scenarios played out on a daily basis, tomorrow would be different. The only question was how different and what would the new day bring? If I could have foreseen the future, would I have done things any differently? The drama to come was not worth all the money in the world, trust me!

# 7

# BIG SISTA

"Learn to fail or fail to learn."

Over a very short period of time, Beverly and Tamika had bonded more than I could have ever imagined. I could only attribute their connection to the universal law of opposite attracts. Tamika's hard, undisciplined lack of structure and culture, gave way to Beverly's very structured and almost anal drive for perfection and poise. The two girls were inseparable after a while. In an unforeseen way, it really helped Beverly as well. She developed a sister-like relationship she had never experienced as an only child. Not only that, but her perception of the local Atlanta girls was dispelled. Up until now, she had been exposed to the worst that Atlanta had to offer. Most of her classmates were out-of-state students.

Beverly was also able to open up to Tamika about the brutal killing of her father. This was such a milestone for Beverly. She had not been able to open up about such a personal loss to anyone. In return, Tamika felt secure enough to talk about her own past experiences of sexual and physical abuse in foster homes throughout her childhood. The two girls spent much of their time crying and laughing together. Beverly turned out to be such a great influence on Tamika that she went from an occasional casual drug user to not using at all. Beverly also felt it very rewarding knowing the positive effects that her presence was having on Tamika. They spent countless hours going to the malls and Atlanta's eateries.

Just as fast as Tamika had fallen into that dark place of drugs, alcohol and partying, she emerged into the light. The contrast was like night and day, from the girl I had my one-man intervention with. What a difference two months had made! I had arranged for Derrick to be her assigned driver over these two months so our interaction had been mostly phone conversations.

On this day, the weather was so nice that I suggested we meet down at Piedmont Park. I pulled up to the entrance of the park at Tenth and Charles Allen and to my amazement a car was pulling out of its parking spot at the very same moment. Parking at Piedmont Park on a nice day was very much coveted. You typically would have to circle the block three or four times before you would luck up with a parking space. I guessed *The Secret* was working for me. I parked and started scanning the area for Tamika. Five minutes earlier I had received a text from Tamika simply saying, "I'm here."

Walking towards the entrance, I could see a caramel figure in a bright pink sundress. I could not make out if it was Tamika or not because this person's sunglasses covered a large part of her face. Those legs had helped me in my decision to walk in that direction. A few inches higher and that sundress would have had to be called a mini-dress. Her legs kind of strutted from underneath her skirt into some matching pink sandals with a short heel. As I got closer, a familiarity revealed itself when she raised her sunglasses to look at me. It was indeed Tamika.

Damn! She looked good. I was only a few feet away when she ran into my arms.

"Czar, it seem like I have not seen you in like forever."

We stood there in each other's embrace for a moment. I took in her essence. It was surely Beyoncé's perfume Heat. It meshed well with her own body's chemistry. I pushed her away from my body still holding her by her elbows to scrutinize her from head to toe.

"Wow, you look great Tamika."

"You likey?"

"I very much do babe."

Tamika had put back on the weight she had lost and that smile in her words was back. We just aimlessly began to walk into the park, not going anywhere in particular, just wanting to catch up with each other's lives.

"Where should I start Czar?" Tamika started, sighing then taking a deep breath as if her soul was overwhelmed with joy. "First off, I want to really thank you for connecting me with Beverly. She's like the big sister I never had. She has done nothing but feed positive things into my life. I look back at my attitude and the way I carried myself and I'm a little ashamed of who I was—excuse me, whom I was. That's something that Beverly taught me when referring to myself in the past tense. I don't hang out with Princess and Cherry anymore either. They were nothing but bad news. After seeing what drugs did to my mother, I don't believe that I started to use as well. It all started so innocently. Czar, you have no idea how fast I started to spiral down."

"Oh, I could imagine Tamika."

"Some mornings I woke up and could not function until I did a line of cocaine or hit a blunt. I've been totally drug-free since hooking up with Beverly. I'm not going to lie, the desire and temptation comes and goes, but I fight it every time."

We made a left to cross the bridge over the pond in the park. There were a few people with fishing poles cast into the water. Several families of ducks lay on the banks and swam in the pond. Couples walked hand-in-hand to the right and left of us. Atlantans were certainly taking full advantage of this beautiful day in the park. We crossed the bridge and headed past the kiddy playground.

Tamika continued with her testimonial. "Czar, I felt like I was in a haze not knowing if I was coming or going for a while there. Beverly goes on and on about how much she appreciates me listening to her about the murder of her father. I was trying to explain to her that that's the least I could do. She has offered me a whole new lease on life. I'm seriously thinking on going back to school. Beverly said since I have my G.E.D. she would help me with some college prep classes. Could you imagine that, me in college?"

"Yeah, I could Tamika. It's like this Tamika. Fail to learn or learn to fail. From day one I could tell that you were pretty sharp."

"Even with my smart mouth, Czar?"

We both busted out laughing at the candor in her comment. "Yes, even with that smart-ass mouth."

"Do you realize that I would be the first one in my family to attend college?"

"Wow, that would be some accomplishment to be proud of!"

Tamika stopped me in front of what seemed to be the largest and oldest tree in the park. She took my hand, looked me deeply in my eyes and said, "I see what you were trying to do for me from the start."

"What was that Tamika?"

"You were trying to discourage me from this life from day one."

"What you talking about Tamika? I'm about my bottom line."

"You can drop the act Czar. What you don't want anyone to know is that you have a soft side."

I let her hand go and started walking again. "I just knew that this was not for you, Tamika."

"I'll be honest with you Czar, after you took me on that first call I was excited about the money that I made. But after I was alone by myself, I laid the money out on my bed and I was looking at it, next thing you knew I was in tears balled up on the bed next to that dirty, dirty money. I had no idea where all that crying came from. It was not just about me taking that first call. It felt as if all my past pain just came to the surface in that instant: the sexual molestation, physical abuse, abandonment and the emotional void in my life. I cried and cried then the next morning I got high for the first time with a client. I realize that getting high made it easier to take calls. I numbed myself to the reality of my life."

"Well Tamika, what brought on the change?"

"Well, to be honest, I remembered what you said that day you took me to lunch."

"What was that?"

"Your words were 'True change begins in your heart then in your mind and eventually it would show in your life.' Do you remember saying that to me?"

"Yeah, of course I do."

"Well, those words really resonated with me."

"Reso- what? You really beginning to sound like Beverly now."

"To be honest with you, up until a week ago I did not really know what *resonated* meant."

"Well, that's what learning is all about; there's nothing to be ashamed of. Let me be the first to tell you that your change is showing all over that dress you're wearing."

Tamika blushed and playfully punched me on my arm. We walked in silence for a while just soaking in the beautiful weather and scenery. The park was filled with all sorts of activities: kids riding bikes, kite's being flown, in-line skaters, joggers and a multitude of couples, hand-in-hand. We walked past a couple sitting on a park bench sharing a tender kiss. Tamika looked away from the couple and right into my eyes. It was a bit awkward for me and I guess it showed in my demeanor.

"Don't worry, I don't want you to hold my hand or kiss me Czar." She was visibly upset and not joking.

"Tamika, where did that come from?"

She started walking ahead of me, arms now folded.

"TAMIKA! TAMIKA, hold on a sec." I had to put a slight jog into my walk to catch up to her. I caught up to her, grabbed her by her arms to turn her to face me, and that's when I saw it. Her eyes were welled up with tears.

"Look Czar, I'm just ready to go. Forget about what I said and let's just leave."

"No, let me know if it's something that I did."

Passersby were now looking at the small scene that Tamika and I were creating. I heard two female joggers run past and whisper, "Girl, don't let no man make you cry."

I turned my attention back to Tamika. "Yo, what's really good with you Tamika?"

"Well Czar, if you really want to know, I'm tired of throwing myself at you and you continuously shoot me down. Can you deny that there was something between us in that room before you just turned me over to Malik and Derrick? What about the day we had lunch at the Thai restaurant and you came around and opened the door to let me into the car?"

In the most sensitive voice I could muster, I said, "Look Tamika, that's just second nature for me to open doors and pull out chairs."

"Well I ain't never had… excuse me, I have never had a man open any doors nor pull out any chairs for me. You running around here fucking everybody else but me! What's wrong with me? Tell me. Tell me what's wrong with my pussy? I was on the phone with Diamond the other day and I had to listen to her talk about how good you ate her pussy and then the dick was the bomb, and on and on. I had to cut our conversation short simply because I did not want to hear the details of you making some other bitch cum." Tamika was talking way too loudly—loud enough to get a few snickers and giggles from the people within earshot of us.

"Come on Tamika, let's walk and talk."

She continued, "I know I look way better than Diamond. She's cool and all but what do you see in her that I don't have? She's a hoe just like me, so what is it? You don't want to be seen in public or holding hands with a whore, is that it?" At this point I was so clear that Tamika's outburst had absolutely nothing to do with me. It surely was misplaced aggression. She wanted affection and attention from the first person who ever really treated her humanely.

Reaching for her hand then letting our fingers interlock, I responded, "I have no problem with holding your hand in public Tamika."

Her face lit up and she composed herself while drying her tears with her free hand. "I'm sorry Czar. I feel so stupid. You only known me for a short time and I've cried on your shoulders way too much."

I just chuckled at that fact, still listening to her. "I've never had anyone be nice to me without wanting something in exchange, and more times than not, they want my body so I'm programmed to equate affection with sex. So when you reject me I feel like there is nothing else that I can offer you than sex."

"Tamika, there was something about you from day one. I don't know exactly what it was but I think you're pretty special."

"It's hard for me to tell that you think that."

"Well, I really do. Tamika when you meet the right guy he's going to engage and stimulate your mind before he gets anywhere near your body."

"Well, I know a guy like that!" she replied, biting her bottom lip flirtatiously. "Do you?"

"You never stop trying, do you? When you have your scope on something you get tunnel vision, huh? I can appreciate your persistence and tenacity Tamika. Do you know that we were calling you little Miss Persistent when you first started to call the agency for a job."

"No, stop playing."

"Yeah, you did not take no for an answer and you followed up several times with phone calls." We laughed hand-in-hand as we made our way back to my truck to leave the park.

"Czar, I did get the email that you sent me with your poetry. I loved the one titled *Groupie*. I can relate to it on so many levels. 'Champaign and weed in abundance, kept me in a haze of dumbness.' That's the line that sticks out in my head more than anything else. It really made me take a self-evaluation. I think you have a gift with words Czar."

"Wow, thank you for saying that!"

"You actually inspired me to write something as well but I'm not ready to share it with you yet."

"Okay, whenever you get comfortable Tamika, I'd love to hear it."

"Cool!"

### Groupie

You jump in bed with fame, never asking names.

Caught his eyes from the stage, one wink and it's the start of the game.

Your waist sways from side to side, nothing but hips and thighs.

Champaign and weed in abundance, keep you in a haze of dumbness.

Tits and ass still firm, with tomorrow your least concern.

Fellatio connoisseur, your skill art got them coming back for more.

A harlot with the spirit of lust, men fall victim to your touch.

In and out, up and down you're the one they pass around.

Safe, unsafe it doesn't matter, moans of his voice is what you treasure.

Promiscuous and alone, the lights and camera are gone when you're at home.

"Maybe he'll be different from the rest," I did swallow his seed which I digest.

Tempted by the shiny apple, your soul belongs to the social circle.

A beautiful outer shell, it's a shame your spirit belongs to HELL...

By, Ceasar Mason

We got back to the truck and I came around to open up her door. Jokingly she said, "Look, you going to confuse a girl with all your chivalry and shit."

Tamika had a great sense of humor. As we sat there in the parked truck Tamika reached down on the middle console of the truck and pulled out an orange box cutter. Mocking my Brooklyn accent, she said, "Yo son, who face you going to chop with this? Or excuse me, who you going to give a buck fifty to?" Coming out of character for a second, she asked, "Isn't that what they call it? A buck fifty?"

Laughing, I replied, "Shorty, you crazy as hell."

Tamika pushed the blade up and you could hear its trademark sound, a series of clicking sounds. That sound brought back memories or nightmares depending on what side of the blade you were on. When you heard that sound on the Number 3 or 4 trains in Brooklyn it only meant problems.

Tamika continued playing with the box cutter. "Czar, can I have it?"

"What are you going to do with a box cutter?"

"I'm going to start taking it on calls with me."

"I don't really advise that. Statistically, weapons of protection are usually turned against you by a perpetrator."

"I need to have something when I go in on these calls."

"What do you think me and the other dudes are for?"

"I need something right then and there." Tamika was making a compelling argument.

I finally relinquished, "You can keep it Mami."

She immediately stuffed it in her purse.

Pulling into traffic, I asked her where she was heading.

"I may be going over to Beverly's house. Let me call her."

Beverly had just gotten in from a date and wanted both Tamika and I to come by to tell us all about him.

When we got over to Beverly's place she opened the door and rushed into my open arms. We had not seen each other in some considerable amount of time as well. After releasing me from her grips, she playfully hugged Tamika with as much zest, mockingly since she had just been with her earlier that morning. The two girls hugged as if they had not seen each other in an eternity.

We stepped into Beverly's apartment where she made a beeline to her blender that had ice, alcohol and daiquiri mix already in it. All she had to do was push the button which she did. She brought out our drinks which were garnished with orange slices and whole cherries. We settled in her living room where Tamika sat next to Beverly on the sofa and I sat directly across from both of them on the loveseat. Beverly's place could only be described as contemporary chic. It was nicely decorated. Less was really more.

I opened up the floor for conversation. "Well, let's hear about this new guy you went on a date with."

"Oh my God, I can't tell you the last time I've been on a REAL date like this one. Our line of work is not conducive to dating let me tell you."

I chimed in, "who you telling?"

The two ladies looked at each other, then me. "Now you know you don't have no problem finding no date," they said simultaneously.

"What makes ya'll think that because I'm a man that this job don't pose some of the same dating challenges?" Then, diverting the topic, I said, "Look, it's about your date right now anyway. Please continue."

"Well, his name is Donavan. We met about two weeks ago while I was in Whole Foods. He saw me reaching for something on the top shelf and came over to help me. I took his number and on a whim called him. On the second day of us meeting, I found him to be so interesting. He was born in Jamaica but grew up in Miami. He has been in Atlanta for the last seven years. He's thirty years old, no kids, never been married and can make me laugh like no one's business. After talking every day to each other for the past week he called yesterday and was like, 'You like seafood?' I was like, 'Yeah.' Then he said, 'Well I'll pick you up tomorrow about three o'clock.' Before I knew what I was saying, I was fully complying with his demands. It turned me on so much that he was not asking me to go out; he was telling me and no was not an option. My panties were moist after talking to him."

Tamika acknowledged what Beverly was saying with a high five. "I love a manly man girl!"

Both women were making sure not to spill the contents of their glasses in their hands.

"I was a little reluctant to have him come to my place but I had great intuitions about him. I did not let him come up to the apartment though. So, when I got downstairs he was holding a vase with an assortment of all different color roses and a small gift box. When I tell you guys that I teared up immediately, I was so overwhelmed. That kind of courtship is so dead in this city and most large cities across the country. I could have been knocked over with a feather at this point. He opened the car door for me. He's such a gentleman."

In that instant, Tamika flashed me a telling smile without Beverly noticing it. Beverly continued with the details of her date. "I sat the flower on the floor in the back seat and opened my small gift-wrapped box. It was a bottle of Gwenn Stefani perfume *Lamb.* How he knew that it was one of my favorite fragrances is beyond me. At this point I had no idea where we were going to eat. He wouldn't say; all I knew was it was a seafood place. After driving a short distance to Peachtree Street, we pulled into the parking deck which housed the Oceanaire Restaurant. Donavan had really good taste. His Jamaican accent emphasizes the B in Beverly. Every time he said my name it made me smile. Dinner could not be better—the food was good but the conversation with Donavan was even better. Topics of discussion ranged from politics, social issues, family values, you name it. Donavan was such a breath of fresh air for me tonight."

Tamika interjected, "What does he do for a living?"

"He drives trucks, not over the road but here locally. He's not rich or anything like that but he's so attentive to me not to mention easy on the eyes. He dropped me back home and I was waiting for the sexual advances but they never came. He leaned in for a hug and a soft kiss on the cheek. It's been a long time since anyone has made me feel like that. Can you believe it, a real date, and here in Atlanta to boot? Men in Atlanta have way too many options and are way too spoiled; they don't want to put in the work to get to know a woman."

Tamika jumped in, rolling her eyes. "That's why if they not paying, I'm not playing. Simple as that!"

"That's cool, Beverly. I'm really happy for you. There may be some possibilities with (in my best Jamaican accent) Mr.

Yardman." We all laughed at the moniker I put on Donavan and my cheesy Jamaican accent.

"Thank you Czar, it's only the first date so we'll see how things progress."

"That's a healthy attitude. Just enjoy yourself without any expectations."

"Well, enough about me and my date. What have you guys been up to?"

There was a thunderous silence then a moment when both Tamika and I attempted to avert eye contact with each other. Even though there was nothing going on between us, our actions did nothing to dispel that there wasn't. Our muteness created a sly smirk on Beverly's face. She certainly was formulating her own pictures in her head. It was Tamika who spoke up first.

"Me and Czar just met at Piedmont and walked around a little."

"Oh, okay so you and Czar were just strolling hand-in-hand in Piedmont Park on a nice sunny day!" Beverly's words were laced with sarcasm and suggestiveness, with a matter-of-fact look on her face and tone in her voice. She then turned her gaze to me as if to say, "What's your version of the time in the park with Tamika?"

"Beverly, me and Tamika just needed to catch up. We had not seen each other in a while. To be honest, most of the conversation was about you."

"ME!"

"Yes you. Tamika was gushing about how much of a great influence you've been in her life in such a short period of time. You got her thinking about going back to school."

Beverly corrected me. "No, not thinking about going back, she's going to do it." They both exchanged smiles of confirmation. "The truth of the matter is that Tamika has been just as much a blessing in my life as well. She's like a sponge that wants better for herself. She never had the environment that could cultivate all that she is in a positive way." The two women were face to face. They leaned in and hugged one another. Muffled from the long embrace, Beverly managed to say, "She makes it so easy to be a big sister to her."

I sat across from them and just listened as they edified each other back and forth. The sincere gratitude and love between the both of them was very much evident. I rose to my feet and walked to the kitchen where I placed my now empty daiquiri glass in the sink.

Upon returning to the living room, I said, "Ladies, it's been fun but I have to go."

Tamika must have been reading my mind. "Czar I'm good here for the night. Me and Beverly have some girly things to talk about."

Beverly could not resist but to go there one last time. "Listen, for the record I think you two make a really cute couple."

Tamika and I just stood there looking at each other. She and her legs looked just as good as they did in that dress in the earlier part of the day. Beverly's mouth was moving and I was sure she was talking but I could not hear any of her words. Tamika and I were locked in on each other. It was only for about thirty seconds or so but it felt much, much longer. The only thing that could stop Beverly's chatter was her ringing phone. She turned and ran toward it.

"I'm sure that's your Yardman!" I taunted.

She retreated into her bedroom for some privacy.

Now that we were alone in the room, Tamika came closer and said, "Thank you for the walk in the park and not taking advantage of my vulnerability."

Looking at her, I said, "I had just as much fun as you did."

"I'm really digging your swag Czar."

I blushed and thanked her. "I dig your style as well."

Tamika reached in for an innocent hug and it was at that very moment Beverly came back into the room from her phone call.

"And ya'll acting like there's nothing going on, huh?"

Tamika stepped back away from me.

"Ladies, I'm out." Beverly ran over to hug me good-bye and with that, I exited her apartment.

Beverly must have heard the sense of urgency in Tamika's voice when she said she wanted to stay and have girl chat because as soon as I left, she turned to Tamika and asked, "Is everything okay Tamika?"

Tamika walked over to the sofa and beckoned Beverly to sit down. "Beverly, I can't continue living like this! This business has changed me in so many ways it's not funny."

"Girl! I totally feel you right now. It's like you're reading my mind. It's funny that you brought it up but I've been feeling strongly about getting out of the life as well. This is my last year in school. I'll be graduating soon. My plan was to get my degree and get out into the job market and act like none of this ever happened. Today while I was out on the date with Donavan I sat across from him and looked at his great big smile and nice teeth and thought to myself, how would he feel if he knew what I did? I felt like I was living a lie. No man is going to want to turn a hoe into a housewife."

Tamika nodded in agreement and added, "We need to come up with an exit plan sis. We can't do this shit forever."

"I totally agree with you. What do you propose?"

"I actually had been talking to one of my clients who's been investing in real estate for years now. If we go hard for the next several months we could come up with seed money together quicker than we can separately. He was explaining to me that it's a buyers' market right now. We could buy properties as low as forty cents on the dollar right now."

"I'm impressed with you little sis."

Tamika was beaming from the adoration of her big sister. She continued. "I have some money saved up. I'm going to get that convertible CLK because paying those drivers to take us on calls is cutting into our bottom line."

"You know it girl." The two ladies giggled and slapped each other five. Beverly had an afterthought! "But don't you like to know that we have protection right outside of a call?"

"Man, these tricks ain't about to do nothing crazy, trust me!"

"Did you hear about the girl Cherry?"

"Beverly, those are rare occasions that you can count on one hand." Tamika walked over to her purse and reached in. She pulled out her orange box cutter to show Beverly for illustrative purposes. She pushed the blade out. It made a menacing clicking sound. "This is what I'm going to do to the muthafuckers that step out of line with me." Tamika slashed wildly at the air as if to demonstrate.

"Where did you get that?"

Tamika stopped slashing her imaginary victim long enough to answer, "From Czar!" then went back to slashing.

"That figures! He be on some real New York shit."

As if something jogged her memory, Tamika excitedly yelled, "Guess what?"

"What Tamika!"

"I'm moving downtown to Atlantic Station next week right on Seventeenth Street."

"Girl, that's what's up. You're going to be right in the center of everything."

"You know it."

"I'm really proud of how you're taking control of your life Tamika. You don't need drugs and alcohol to have a good time."

"I know that now thanks to you and Czar. You're such an inspiration to me Beverly."

"Right now, you're the inspiration to me, lil' sista, coming up with that great plan focusing on making your money. I guess it's a two way street with us. I'm about to refocus much harder on making my money too. I have this client… well, he's not exactly a typical client per say. It's more of a sugar daddy relationship that Czar had set me up with outside of the agency. His name is Jonathan Weilz II."

"Is he white?"

"Yeah, he's white and very wealthy."

"Well, what's the problem then?"

"He is so controlling and into bondage, strap on and all sorts of sadomasochistic shit, that turns my stomach."

"A real freak, huh!"

"He's been pressing me to see him more regularly but it's hard for me to be around him with a straight face sometimes."

"Is it that bad?"

"Yes, it's that bad. He inherited his money from his father and loves getting his own way. He's a spoiled little child in an adult's body." Both girls laughed at Beverly's comment.

"Girl, do what you have to do and keep your mind's eyes on the prize."

"Which is?"

"Well, you want to be in a real relationship with Donavan right!"

"Yeah, absolutely."

"Well, we have to get out of this trap of selling our bodies sooner than later, girl!"

"What's your motivation Tamika?"

"What do you mean?"

"What's the prize that your mind's eyes are focusing on?"

"I simply want better for myself. I don't ever want to go back to that 'hood existence I grew up knowing, mentally nor physically. I want to be able to travel the world and see some of the places you've seen."

"You like Czar don't you?"

A sheepish smile came across Tamika's face as she was posed with the question. Was it that obvious? She laughed to herself. "Czar is cool as fuck, I'm really feeling him! Have you ever been with him?"

"Like have sex? Oh no, he took me under his wing as his little sister from the day we met. He was very supportive when I told him that my father was murdered and the circumstances that led me to escorting." Beverly's voice just trailed off by the thought of her father's death then she snapped back out of her reflective thoughts and said, "Czar's looking for an out as well."

"I get that impression too Beverly. He's way different than the typical guy out here."

"Yeah, he is. Let's put this plan in motion sis."

"Let's do it."

# 8
# JONATHAN WEILZ II

"A million dollars inherited does not
have the same value as a million dollars earned."

Jonathan Weilz senior grew up in Hungary during the Nazi occupation. He assumed a Christian identity to escape prosecution. In an ironic twist of fate, the then teenage Jonathan Weilz would be hired to help loot the properties and treasures of his fellow Jews. He took control of large estates and all of their possessions. Jonathan sat idle and watched many of his Jewish friends slaughtered and shipped off to death camps such as Auschwitz. Young Jonathan rose in rank through the chain of command quickly. He had impressed his superiors so much that he was elevated to head up the Nazi Economic Department in Hungary at an early age. What his superiors did not know was that he had secretly amassed a small fortune for himself in the process. In an effort of pure self-preservation, Jonathan had lost any and all integrity that he may or may not have had. He was a lascivious creature that turned his back on his fellow Jews for silver and gold. He would later be quoted as saying, "The normal rules don't apply. You have to forget how you behave in a normal society. This is an abnormal situation."

After the war, like many other high ranking Nazi officers, Jonathan fled Europe in fear of arrest and execution for war crimes and crimes against humanity. Jonathan Weilz senior had the classic American immigrant story, coming through Ellis Island with the tens of thousands of others looking for a better life for themselves and their families. The thing that separated him from all the other immigrants that were seeking fortune and happiness was that he was already a wealthy man. True to his disciplines, he went into finance. New York City the capital of the world's financial district would be the perfect backdrop for Jonathan Weilz to flourish and that he did! Jonathan became a staple in the social circle with New York City's rich and elite. He was well known as a wealthy playboy, courting the attention of some of Hollywood's beautiful starlets. His sexual exploits were legendary not just in New York but in all the hot cities: Los Angeles, Miami and Las Vegas to name a few. Eyebrows raised when it was announced via a full page ad in the New York Times, *Millionaire Playboy To Wed Big Screen Actress*. Everyone publicly bestowed their blessings and well wishes but whispered their doubts among each other in private.

Surprisingly, married life gave Jonathan senior the direction and stability for which he was crying out. His philandering ways did not cease, they just subsided, which was quite fine with his socialite wife who spent way too much time shopping and spending his money to notice. They had a toleration for each other with an unspoken understanding. The public image of the couple was that of a fairytale; no one suspected anything other than marital bliss. It was years later that Mrs. Weilz bore him an heir. All who did not believe in the reformed playboy charades persona, would certainly be convinced when once again a grand announcement was declared of the pending pregnancy. In the hospital on the day of the delivery, Jonathan was elated to learn of the birth of his healthy son. The Weilz name would live on in spite of the fact that all of his family had been exterminated at the hands of Hitler's third Reich. He carried the burden of guilt for much of his life. Even though he was not under any threat by being Jewish in the new world, he continued as a pseudo-Christian. He would raise his new heir, Master Jonathan Weilz II, as a Christian as well. In his mind, he felt a degree of vindication with the birth of his son. He would pray for years to come that his sins would not bear evident in his son's life. Even as a pretend Christian he knew the verse that read, "The sins of the father is visited upon the son."

Jonathan Weilz II had a fairytale upbringing. He had a life of chauffeurs and nannies; he attended the most prestigious private schools in New York; he was showered with elaborate gifts and spectacular birthday parties. In his parent's eyes, young Master Jonathan could do no wrong even when he did. In his early teens he would regularly get caught torturing the family's dog or cat. They dismissed his actions as a phase which he would grow out of. He seldom or never was disciplined for his bad behavior. He acted out in school moreso than anywhere else. Bullying his male classmates and inappropriately touching his female classmates went unaddressed on a regular basis. The school was not about to expel the son of their largest endowment contributor for such "silly adolescent expression" as they referred to it. His actions were borderline criminal; at least misdemeanors. By the time Jonathan was sixteen he had already grown to six feet and weighed two hundred pounds, which made bullying all the more easier. Jonathan was a C average student at best but he did excel in sports. He played basketball, football, tennis and even fencing.

His mother noticed an unsettling nervousness about their housekeeper, Carmen, whenever young Jonathan was around.

Carmen had lost that smile in her voice and on her face that Jonathan's mother had come to love seeing. Something was surely wrong. Carmen and her two sisters had immigrated from Panama ten year's earlier and found work as domestic help for the wealthy Upper East Side New York families. Carmen was thirty-three years old, five-foot-four, slender and curvaceous. The black and white maid uniform looked more like a novelty costume that a playful wife would put on to entice her husband. That full size C-cup of hers nestled together and protruded at the opening of her neckline. The hem of her skirt dropped right above her knees. Those tan toned legs could have belonged to a world class gymnast. She had a dark bronze complexion from her native Panama. Carmen wore her long shoulder-length jet black hair in an unassuming ponytail. Her thick black eyebrows matched her hair; it gave her a soft younger-than-she-was appearance.

Carmen had been with the Weilz family for the past five years and played a larger role in the rearing of young Jonathan. Typically, Carmen would be the first face that he saw when she awoke him and fixed his breakfast. She was also the last person he saw in the late evening after dinner. Both his parents were still quite the socialites even in their older age. His mother had not forgotten how to spend money extravagantly nor did his father's libido subside for beautiful upcoming stage actresses. Jonathan senior only learned a lot more discretion with his mistresses in his maturity; he was still the quintessential playboy of yester years on the inside. Needless to say, neither parent spent much time with young teenage Jonathan.

Two years prior, when Jonathan was just fourteen but still a towering figure over Carmen, she had entered his room after dinner to place his freshly-ironed khaki slacks, white button-up shirt and navy blue oxford-style blazer uniform in his room for the following school day. Carmen tapped lightly on the door before entering. This was a ritual performed night after night, but this night would be different from the rest. With no answer she assumed that Master Jonathan was asleep. She quietly pushed the door open and tip-toed into the room, placing the uniform on the hook which was on the back of the closet door.

On the way out of the room she heard a faint voice calling her name, "Carmen!"

She looked over at the covered-up lump on the bed that was Master Jonathan. "Yes, Master Jonathan."

"Come over here Carmen."

Without hesitation, Carmen walked to his bedside. Surely he needed her help with something. Jonathan sprang up stalk naked and grabbed Carmen by the throat. Before she knew it, she was on the bed beneath his massive weight. His hands were over her mouth to prevent her from screaming. His silhouette was purely black but she could make out the white in his eyes in the dark room. With his hands still covering her mouth he began to talk in a whisper. "Carmen, I like you and I want to have you. Do you like me?"

Carmen could only shake her head no.

"I'm very disappointed to hear that. Do you like working here?"

He did not give her a chance to answer. His free hand was pulling down her stockings and hiking up her short uniform dress. Jonathan continued whispering into Carmen's ear while on top of her. "I'm sure you like being in this country. My father is a very wealthy and powerful man. How would you feel if you and your sisters were deported because you chose to mistreat a teenage boy from an affluent family, huh?"

At this point he could feel her body relax under him; she was no longer tense. She would not fight off his advances any more. "Good."

He knew that he could now remove his hand from over her mouth. He took his erect penis and brutally thrust himself into her. Carmen had not been with a man in several years now; she truly was a good Catholic woman. Jonathan attempted to kiss her lips. She moved side to side, preventing his lips from touching hers. That degree of intimacy caused Carmen's stomach to curl at the thought of kissing him in the mouth. Jonathan gave up and settled for suckling on her firm, proportioned breasts. Jonathan continued raping her for what seemed like eternity to Carmen. She could only reach for her rosary bead necklace around her neck. She clasped onto the cross pendant for dear life and closed her eyes. She heard him let out a loud moan of pleasure then he got off of her. She could do nothing but lay there.

The sound of his voice broke both the silence between them and the shock-type trance that she was in. "Now that was not so bad, was it?"

Carmen managed to lift herself to her feet and began gathering her things while walking out the room. Jonathan was snickering something under his breath that she could not make out. To Carmen, the whole scene seemed surreal like a bad dream or nightmare. Carmen was certain that this was not the first time he had raped someone. He was just a little too comfortable violating her. And it would not be the last time that he would rape her either.

Over the next two years, he would periodically have his way with Carmen. Every time was more brutal than the last. Once he even held his fencing sword inches from her neck in an attempt to instill fear and control. He was also getting bolder and bolder in his actions. The rape was no longer just exclusive to nights in his room. He would risk his parents catching him in the mornings and during the day while they were at home as well. She sensed that the idea of possibly getting caught gave him that much more of a rush to do it and take the chance. He kept her prisoner by the thought of her and her sisters returning to the poverty that they had been part of growing up in Panama.

Two years of holding this threat over Carmen's head was about to come to an abrupt end! It was only a matter of time for it to be found out since Carmen was now three months pregnant with her sixteen-year-old rapist's baby. How would she explain this to her family? Would she be the reason for her sisters being deported? What would Jonathan do if he found out? Would he physically harm her? Like most rape victims, she started blaming herself for what had taken place.

She had started working for the Weilz family when Jonathan was just eleven years old. She found him initially so adorable but knew they were raising a beast shortly after that. She witnessed him do things without admonishment for any of his actions. He was simply a spoiled brat that wanted things his way and he had learned over the years that he could do as he pleased without reproach.

Mrs. Weilz really cared about and admired Carmen. She knew in her heart that she could not do half of what Carmen did on a daily basis: cooking, cleaning, food shopping and running the family errands. Yes, she was thankful for Carmen and paid her well in exchange. She could tell that Carmen was visibly shaken and not herself for some time now. Carmen was not just a housekeeper to her; after five years she was like family. Mrs.

Weilz did not know how true that thought was of Carmen being family!

On this day, it was now late morning and Mr. Weilz Senior was at the office and Jonathan was off to school. The tension in the kitchen was so thick it could be cut with a knife and not even a sharp one. Carmen avoided any eye contact with Mrs. Weilz in fear of being found out. It was way too late for that. Mrs. Weilz broke the ice first.

"Carmen, why don't you fix two cups of tea and sit with me for a moment?"

"Yes, Mrs. Weilz." Carmen squeezed lemon and sweetened both cups of tea with one sugar then sat down next to Mrs. Weilz. There was a quiet while both women took an initial sip of their tea.

Mrs. Weilz was not known for beating around the bush. "Carmen is everything okay at home?"

"Si, I mean yes, Ma'am."

"Then why do I have the notion that something is so very wrong with you?"

Carmen could not contain herself any longer. The water welled up in her eyes and as if a dam had levied, she busted out uncontrollably crying. Mrs. Weilz leaned in and held her on her shoulders. "Dear, dear child let it out. Let it all out!"

Carmen composed herself and pushed away from her arms. She just sat staring blankly at Mrs. Weilz while the words formulated in her head.

"What is it Carmen? What's the problem? Let me help you."

Then, like the dam that breaks, she blurted out, "Jonathan raped me and he has been raping me for the past few years."

Thank God Mrs. Weilz was already seated because the words struck her like a ton of bricks. Her natural motherly instincts went into auto pilot. "No, not my Jonathan, not my boy. Jonathan may be a little mischievous but he would never do something like this."

Tears were now coming down both women's faces. Even though Mrs. Weilz was vehemently denying her son's actions with her mouth, in her heart she knew that Carmen was indeed telling the truth. She started blaming herself. How could she have given him everything except integrity, honor and virtue? Those things could not be bought because they were simply priceless.

"Carmen, what can we do to make this unpleasant situation go away?"

Carmen held up her slumped shoulder and raised her head to answer Mrs. Weilz. "What do you mean ma'am?"

"Well this is about money right? Isn't that usually the case with you people?" Mrs. Weilz got up to walk to the home office to get out her checkbook but was stopped dead in her tracks when Carmen also rose to her feet.

In a tone she had never heard Carmen speak in the five years that she had employed her, Carmen replied, "Do you think I want your money?" It was filled with pride and dignity.

"Well, why else would you be boo-hooing like you are?"

"I clean your toilets and floors because I want to earn my living. I cannot marry a rich man that I don't love."

"What are you suggesting Carmen, that I don't love my husband? It goes without saying that you are certainly fired! Please get your things and leave."

Carmen had yet to drop the bomb on Mrs. Weilz. A tearful Carmen pleaded through her crying and muttering words. All of her fears were coming to life now. Drying her face and collecting herself, Carmen managed the words, "I'm PREG-NANT!!"

"What did you say?"

"I said I was pregnant!"

Mrs. Weilz gripped onto the chair to steady herself. She did not see that coming when she awoke this morning. It was a different ballgame now and she knew it. Carmen now held all the chips. "Carmen, please sit down. I need to call Mr. Weilz at the office and let him know that we have pressing family business here at home that he needs to tend to." Mrs. Weilz was more overwhelmed at the ensuing scandal that this would stir up amongst the Upper East Side crust. It was totally unacceptable to have babies with the "hired help."

Mrs. Weilz returned from making the phone call to her husband who assured her that he'd be on his way immediately. They both sat at the table with their unfinished tea which was now cold.

"How many months are you Carmen?"

"I am three months now."

"Good, good, we have a physician upstate about one hour away that can fix this whole situation."

"What do you mean Mrs. Weilz?"

"I'm referring to an abortion!"

"I cannot have an abortion Mrs. Weilz."

"Of course you can, why not?"

"I am Catholic, we do not believe in abortion."

"Let's talk about this more when my husband gets here."

"There is nothing to talk about. I cannot take a life."

Carmen was adamant with her decision as to not have an abortion. She came to a mutual agreement with the Weilz that she would leave the state, have the baby and either put it up for adoption or raise it anonymously on her own. She agreed to this with the understanding that they would not attempt to have her and her sisters deported and they would give her an undisclosed sum of money. The case was closed before Jonathan had even returned home from school that day. His father was not convinced that he had raped Carmen. He thought it was consensual and that Jonathan was a teenage boy with raging hormones that had "slipped up." Once again his deeds went unpunished.

A few years later, at the age of eighteen, his mother had not announced herself upon entering the house and found him prancing and parading around in women's underwear with lipstick on. Mrs. Weilz immediately called Dr. Goldstein, a leading psychiatrist in all sorts of disorders. She hoped that her son would finally get the help that he needed.

It was no surprise that when he was accepted to Yale, Jonathan's father sat on one of their boards at the school. During his college years, Jonathan developed a taste for the sauce and smoking pot. He went to school as a social event as opposed to an educational experience. He managed to go through the first three years without any serious incidents.

In his last year of school, he had left a party pretty drunk with a date in his passenger seat. Neither of them was wearing a seatbelt. He crashed the car and fled, leaving his date in his wrecked car bloodied and mangled. She did not die but she would never walk again. She was paralyzed from the neck down. Later on, it was ruled an accident. According to the official police report, Master Weilz had fallen asleep, his grueling late night studying having caught up with him. Jonathan Weilz Sr.

was able to orchestrate this with one simple phone call in the wee hours of the morning. POWER. Jonathan walked away from the accident with minor scratches and abrasions plus no legalities. His passenger and her family never disputed those facts. I wondered why! Jonathan barely graduated. I think they were happier just to see him leave their fine institution of learning.

Upon graduating, Jonathan went to work for his father's finance company. This was short-lived because his blunders and lack of respect for the more experienced partner were a continuous embarrassment for his father and the Weilz name. The senior Mr. Weilz was sincerely tired of his son's exploits and outbursts at the office which was located in the heart of the financial district in New York City for all to see. It was the last straw when Jonathan took a male lover who had worked in the mailroom of his father's firm. There were rumors of midday trysts in his office with his gay lover and little discretion about it. It was not clear as to his sexual preference because he had normal heterosexual relationships and was known to frequent female prostitutes and escorts. Jonathan had just turned into a deviant sex fiend.

Mr. Weilz senior hatched a plan to offer Jonathan a fresh new start and get him away from the meat and potatoes of his business. He had owned a real estate and land acquisition firm for many years in Atlanta, Georgia. The current president decided to take an earlier than expected retirement. He would send Jonathan to fill the chair of new president. Mr. Weilz pitched it to Jonathan as if it was a promotion but in Jonathan's heart of hearts he knew his father was just getting rid of him; he had failed his father yet again. Jonathan had always sought his father's approval as a young boy. He vowed to himself that he would change his father's opinion about him by going to Atlanta and doing a great job and staying out of trouble. The position came with a five bedroom Spanish-style mansion with a three-car garage. It was located in old Buckhead, right off of Mount Paran Road. The position also came with a million dollar sign-on bonus for young Jonathan. He accepted the position and transitioned from New York to Atlanta quietly.

Jonathan was now in his early thirties with a fresh new start, in a new city. It took him no time to find the tempo of the city. Atlanta had the reputation of a party city and it also was one of the major hubs for sex trafficking in the country. The city of Atlanta had the distinction of having more strip clubs per capita than any other city in the United States. There were currently forty existing strip clubs and several pending permits. The city had also issued four thousand dancing permits in the past two years. Jonathan purchased a couple of exotic cars and started learning the Atlanta scene. He was his playboy father reincarnated all over again. They say the apple doesn't fall far from the tree.

Money was never an issue for Jonathan. A million dollars inherited did not have the same value as a million dollars earned. He spent money lavishly in clubs and on the many escorts that he came to know. When he met Beverly she stood out more than the others. There was none like her. Beverly was certainly in it for the money but there were limitations as to what she would do. She did not simply let Jonathan have his way.

For the first time in his life someone had set up boundaries and rules for him to follow. In an ironic twist, these rules and parameters that Beverly had established, were where he found a perverse pleasure of submissiveness. In his everyday life he would be an alpha male, in charge and domineering. Then in his private life he would be able to give up that control and let his Mistress give him orders in a reversal of roles. He found it therapeutic and liberating to be submissive behind closed doors. He felt a degree of comfort with Beverly that he had never felt with any other person. He could see their judgmental stares when he made this "exotic" request of other escorts and this made him uneasy. Beverly just responded more matter-of-factly about his requested services. In some strange way Beverly had tamed him from his previous self. There was something a bit more humane about Jonathan now. It had only been a few months from their initial meeting but their relationship, if you will, veered more towards a sugar-daddy, sugar-baby relationship. Now it was no longer a scenario of Beverly coming over for a few hours and being paid for that time as in a traditional escorting arrangement. Now Jonathan would have a weekly allotted allowance for Beverly and in return she would be way more available to him on a more personable intimate level. We're talking about direct phone calls to Beverly without the agency playing third party, out-of-town trips and vacations, regular lunch and dinner dates. It was like a quasi-relationship without the lying—both fed each other's id openly. Many marriages and relationships are handled based upon these principles and both may be just too ashamed to call it that and admit it; hence the large number of divorces.

Jonathan's subconscious was crying out for domination and discipline—the very things he had lacked all his life growing up.

Beverly became Mistress Beverly and she converted one of his five bedrooms into a training dungeon for Jonathan. The room was painted red and black with chains, handcuffs, and a variety of whips and floggers. In the corner sat medieval-looking apparatuses that were built for a person to get into and have both hands and feet bound and tied. The thing about bondage, or S & M as it's called, is that it's more about control than anything else. Being controlled can create mental stimulation, sexual pleasure or a combination of both. Whatever the reason, Jonathan found an escape and fulfillment in it, but most of all in Beverly.

When the room conversion was completed, both Beverly and Jonathan stood looking at it. Jonathan was aroused by the thought of all of the future experiences that this room would offer him. He stood up behind Beverly and clasped his arms around her. He brought his mouth to her left ear first gently passing his tongue on her lobe. Then he faintly whispered something.

Beverly did not make out what he had said and asked, "What was that?"

Jonathan repeated himself louder and more assured this time. "We need to come up with a SAFE WORD."

Beverly's naivety kicked in. "What's a safe word."

Jonathan cleared his throat as to find the best definition. "Well, a safe word is a word that we come up with that will separate fantasy from reality. When the safe word is voiced, that's the signal to stop."

"Oh, I get it. That's to make sure no one gets a little carried away in the fantasy world, huh."

"Exactly Beverly!"

Beverly excitedly asked, "What should our safe word be?"

Jonathan's eyes went up and to the left; he was being creative. A devilish grin accompanied his answer. "Carmen."

"Carmen! Why Carmen?"

"Let's just say that that name means a lot to me."

Beverly smiled and said, "Carmen it is then."

# 9
# ORANGE BOX CUTTER

"It's best to get caught with it than to get caught without it."

I t had only been two weeks since both Beverly and Tamika had hatched their exit plan. True to her word, Tamika dipped into her stash and bought that Mercedes CLK that she had set her mind on. Now with a car and her condo downtown she was ready to go hard. No more giving up driver's fees for her. She would be able to pad her bottom-line a little better, but at what cost? Everything was in motion, as far as she was concerned.

Beverly on the other hand was tip-toeing around Donavan and her secret lifestyle as an escort. Graduation was approaching soon and Jonathan was being more and more overbearing. Juggling two men was proving to be more difficult than Beverly thought. It was usually Donavan who ended up on the end of broken dinner dates or the recipient of very obvious lies. Jonathan began demanding much more of Beverly, not just of her time but what she wore and what she was doing when they were not together. He felt the more he spent on her, the more say he had in her life. Jonathan would lavish Beverly with shopping sprees and jewelry that she could have cared less about. Jonathan was only mimicking what he saw his father do with his mother as he was growing up. He equated gifts and money with love.

Beverly recalled one such shopping trip to the very same Louis Vuitton store in which she had met Princess and Cherry. She could hear Princess's words echoing in her head. "Girl, why are you out here embarrassing yourself window shopping?" Looking down at the handful of Louis Vuitton shopping bags that she was now carrying brought a smirk to her face. Not only was she now a regular in the store but the manager and salespeople knew her by name. The ironic thing about it all was that she felt worse on the inside than she had felt that day without any bags while window shopping.

Jonathan began suggesting that Beverly quit the service altogether. She totally agreed that she should quit the service. He just did not know that it was not going to be for her to be with him exclusively. Beverly hated being out with Jonathan. She was more conscious of the judgmental stares that she would get in public. It was painfully obvious as to the nature of their relationship to onlookers. The business had not troubled her this much emotionally in the past. Was it because of the love she found in Donavan? Beverly was seeking intimacy so desperately in order to cope with what was going on inside of her. Donavan had been nothing but a gentleman, never pressing her for sex at all. On many occasions she could feel the bulge of his manhood up against her thighs as they embraced and kissed. Beverly had made a sincere connection with Donavan and him with her; living the lie was tortuous to her. She felt unworthy of the flowers and the home-cooked meals he would prepare from his native Jamaica. His rice and peas with oxtails was the tastiest you could ever have had but for apparent reasons it did not go down well for Beverly. Beverly had boyfriends in the past but none like Donavan. Donavan continued with the flowers and the opening of doors and just treated her like his, "Yankee Queen," as he so affectionately called her. The fear of Donavan finding out about her life as a prostitute crippled her with fear. Not fear that he may hit her but fear of losing him. Even though he had never showed her a violent side he wouldn't be wrong for kicking her "Bombo rass."

While Beverly sorted out matters of the heart, Tamika was going a hundred miles and running. She called the office and let them know that she would be on call twenty-four/seven. She had a now or never attitude. When Tamika was not taking calls, she could be found luxuriating in one of the many spas that Atlantic Station had to offer. This new world of super-pampering was so different from the 'hood existence that she had known all of her life. She grew accustomed to the eyebrow arching, manicures, pedicures, bikini waxing and the hot stone massages. Yes. This was the life for her. Luxuriating replaced the drinking and drugging. Tamika had been clean and sober for several months now. She really began loving herself in an honest way. Most women that sold their bodies just did not hold themselves in high esteem. Tamika started to see her own self-worth. She also took up writing poetry as a hobby. It was not clear if she sincerely had a passion for it or if it was a way to get next to Czar. Whatever her reason, she did have skills and she poured out some very deep emotions onto paper, like the one she titled, "Black Girl Lost." It was certainly a mirror of what she was feeling on the inside.

<u>Black Girl Lost</u>

Abandoned at birth, never understanding my worth; never asking why, sometimes I just cry.

Single parent household, why was I disowned? Father never there, why does my heart care?

Momma found solace in a syringe, which she uses to poke her skin.

My body begins maturing in my early teens; men who are supposed to be protectors are being obscene. I want to cover up, but why? Now I'm courting attention of all the guys.

Learn to trade cum for currency, my body is now a commodity.

NASDAQ nor Wall Street got anything on me; you don't lay in my sheets for free.

Materialism and wealth it's all about how money spent.

My policy is offering intimacy without the intricacy.

Never grew up with spirituality, so I let strange men penetrate my dignity.

It doesn't even feel good at the time; this is how I earn my dime.

Men promises comforted this fool; now they'll play by my rules.

Lacking virtue was the cost; I'm just another black girl lost.


By, Tamika McIntosh


Tee knew that Tamika had made herself available to any and all calls. So when she got a call from Antoinette Stein, a successful trial attorney and regular client of the service with a pension for young pretty black girls, she called her. Tamika was in her condo in the middle of fixing a bowl of fresh strawberries and bananas over crème and brown sugar, when her phone rang.

"Hey Tee."

"Are you available for a call?"

"You know I am."

"Well, we have a regular client. She lives in the Mansion high rise on Peachtree Street, right across from Lenox Mall."

"I know exactly where that is but did I hear you right! Did you say SHE!"

"Yeah I did. Is that going to be a problem for you?"

There was silence from Tamika's side of the phone. "No, no that's not a problem at all, it's just I've never seem a female client before. What time did she want me to arrive?"

"In about an hour and a half. Is that enough time for you to get dressed and get over there?"

"Yeah, I'm only like ten to fifteen minutes away from her."

"Mrs. Stein picked you from the website so you don't need to call her or anything. When you get to the building, the valet will park your car. Tell the concierge that you're a guest of Mrs. Stein and he'll let you up." With that said, Tee mentioned that it was a credit card call and she should make sure that she had some credit card slips with her. "Tamika, please check in!" were Tee's last words before hanging up.

Tamika finished her crème and fruit snack then began meticulously putting together what she would wear. She knew a female client would scrutinize her a hundred percent more than a man would. Some men could care less whether she showed up with any clothes on at all. She finally settled for a skirt and blouse that she had gotten from Bebe's the previous day then she finished the ensemble with a pair of sexy Christian Louboutin pumps with a four-inch heel. She sprayed on some of her favorite perfume and she was off.

On the ride over to Mrs. Stein's place Tamika thought of how different it felt. She actually had butterflies of sorts in her stomach. She pulled up to the Mansion, leaving her keys in the still idling car as the valet opened her door. A second gentleman who she suspected was the doorman ushered her into the building to the concierge's desk.

"I'm a guest of Mrs. Stein."

"Yes, yes she's expecting you." The man came around from behind the desk and led her to the elevator. The elevator doors opened up and he slid an access key card into the slot which illuminated the thirty-fifth floor light. "Good day, ma'am."

The elevator whisked her away. It felt like a carnival ride. Everything was all first-class here. Tamika kept wondering, *Who is this lady?* The elevator opened up and Tamika walked to the door. It opened up before she could use the doorbell.

"Hello! And how are you Ms. Innocent?" Before Tamika could answer, the lady chimed on, "Your pictures on the website don't do you justice, darling."

"Thank you Mrs. Stein."

"Please call me Antoinette! You make me sound like an old lady with that Mrs. Stein talk. I love those shoes. Red bottoms no doubt!"

"Yes, you know your shoes," Tamika responded, smiling at the fact she had taken notice of her shoes. At this point, she knew she made a great wardrobe decision. Even though Tamika was answering Antoinette's questions, her eyes were taking in the grandeur of her duplex. This place was easily three thousand square feet of living space. The view faced directly to the front of Lenox Mall.

Antoinette must have been reading her mind. "Great view isn't it?"

"Yes, it is."

"It's really great around Christmas when they light the tree on top of the mall, not to mention fireworks on the Fourth of July and New Year's Day."

The walls had fine art everywhere in between the numerous plaques, diplomas, citations and framed newspaper articles. Who was this lady? Antoinette Stein was five-foot-eight, about one hundred forty-pounds and she radiated wealthy lifestyle. Tamika could not place her ethnicity; she was what some would call racially ambiguous. Her Middle Eastern skin tone could have been from fabulous tanned vacations in the Caribbean. Her facial features could be that of Native American Indian but her hair was shoulder-length and curly. *How did she ever get a name like Stein*, thought Tamika? She was a stunning-looking woman.

As if she was already in tune with Tamika's curiosity, Antoinette said, "Let me show you around."

Tamika was in awe of the place at the end of her tour. She suddenly reminded herself that this was not a social visit. She cleared her throat and politely said, "Tee at the office said that you'll be using a credit card."

"Of course, yes. Sorry, we do need to get that out of the way don't we?" Antoinette replied. She handed Tamika her American Express card and walked to the kitchen while Tamika filled out the credit card slip. Antoinette returned with two glasses of red wine, handed one to Tamika then sat next to her on the loveseat. Tamika had finished filling out the credit card slip and had discretely checked in with the office while Antoinette went into the kitchen. Tamika realized that a female client was way different than male clients. It seemed like female clients were more about making a connection first and foremost. Tamika examined the glass of wine now in her hand; this would be her first drink in quite some time. Tamika thought about how offended drinkers get when others refuse to drink with them. She sat there in that plush apartment thinking about her pervious existence in the West End. The ladies toasted to each other and sat sipping wine chit-chatting.

Between the laughter and playing in each other's hair, Antoinette turned to Tamika and they stared into each other's eyes. They both leaned into each other for a full contact kiss in the mouth. It was long, sensual and soft. Tamika remembered thinking that no man had ever kissed her like that before. She wondered if Czar would ever kiss her that way. Neither woman said a word. Antoinette rose to her feet, took Tamika by the hand and led her up the stairs to her bedroom. They entered the bedroom and both women got onto the bed fully dressed. Undressing each other was part of the experience.

They began by lightly kissing and sucking on each other's neck then Antoinette's blouse came off. Tamika helped her with her bra and out popped the most perfect, symmetrically-shaped C cup she had ever seen—surely store-bought. She reached for the left nipple with her lips while her hands found the right one. Antoinette threw her head back and began to moan with pleasure from Tamika's suckling tongue. Antoinette was now massaging Tamika's pelvis in a slow gentle circular motion.

Cries of "You like!" and "Yes, yes," volleyed between both women.

Tamika began making her way down Antoinette's tussle. She tickled her ribs with her tongue then she found her belly-button which caused Antoinette to giggle. Tamika could feel Antoinette's body trembling with anticipation when her tongue grazed against her cleanly shave clit. She first teased her with long strokes of her tongue while looking her in her eyes from between her legs. Antoinette was now looking back at Tamika, while fondling and kissing her own breast. Tamika took her clit between her two lips as her tongue playfully lashed back and forth across it. Antoinette reached down with her right hand to hold Tamika's head firmly up against her. She began gyrating her midsection feverishly into Tamika's face.

The quiet moans of pleasure gave way to louder outbursts of, "RIGHT THERE, RIGHT THERE! DON'T STOP, RIGHT THERE!"

As Antoinette climaxed, she squirted clear across the room. She found superhuman strength to break away from Tamika's grip. Tamika was astonished and totally surprised by the airborne ejaculation of a woman. She had heard stories of women that did have the ability to squirt but to see it firsthand was amazing. Antoinette lay on her back motionless and exhausted with a smile on her face. Her panting was lessened but you could almost see that her heartbeat was still engaged with the excitement of an orgasm.

Tamika spoke first. "How did you do that?"

"I'll be honest with you. I've only done that four times in my entire life. I think it has more to do with how did you make me do that, than anything! Oh my god, that was great Tamika!"

"I'm glad you liked it."

Antoinette got up then lay down on top of Tamika. She felt obligated to return the favor. Even though Tamika could appreciate Antoinette's gorgeous face and sexy, toned body, being touched by a woman did not really do it for her. Tamika still needed the strong arms, smell and touch of a man. She felt a total relief to know that she was not gay at all, not that she ever questioned it. Antoinette was eating her pussy for what seemed like forever. Tamika wanted to fake it to get it over with. Instead she closed her eyes, relaxed her body and pretended it was Czar down there sucking and licking her kitty. She began giving instructions.

"Curl your index finger upwards and start penetrating the roof of my vagina while you suck on my clit."

Like magic, with the image of Czar in her head and her short cunnilingus tutorial, Tamika could feel the orgasm building up inside her body. It started in her pelvis area then the pulsation moved down to her kitty. Visions of Czar's erect hard chocolate stick penetrating her filled her head and desires. Her pussy began rhythmically throbbing like a heartbeat, faster and faster until she clenched the bed sheets between her fingers in ecstasy. She held his image a little longer thinking about how the real thing would feel. She was tired of hearing about other women's exploits with Czar.

Antoinette was well pleased with herself thinking that she had something to do with Tamika's pleasurable release. Tamika did not take it away from her. Opening her eyes to Antoinette's still-smiling face, she said, "Oh Antoinette, you are good at that!"

"Thank you!"

After a quick shower and a few sprays of Victoria's Secret fragrant body mist, Tamika began getting dressed while Antoinette just sat and admired her. She walked Tamika to the door and said, "I'll certainly be giving the agency a call for you again."

"Okay, I'll be looking forward to it, bye."

"Bye!"

Tamika was back in the car heading down Peachtree on the way back to her condo when her phone rang. She looked at it to see the name "Princess" on the phone screen. Tamika had not been in contact with Princess or Cherry since her sobriety. She was not upset with them or anything, it was just very transparent that they had nothing positive to feed into her life, so she separated herself. Tamika decided to take the call.

"Hey, Princess."

"Hey, my ass. Where you been bitch!"

"A bitch just been about my money."

"I hear that! I also hear you got a little condo downtown and a nice whip too, huh!"

"Yeah, you know those driver fees were adding up, girl."

"Yeah, I know they can. I just copped the new 750 Beamer girl!"

"Oh, those BMW's are nice."

"Yes they are."

Even though on the surface this seemed like a friendly social call to a friend, it was not. Plenty of the girls that were in the sex industry (no matter how beautiful they were on the outside) were very insecure about themselves. They felt that cars, clothes or men validated them. Princess went on and on about how well she was doing and how she went on a recent trip to Las Vegas. In between her words, there were sniffling sounds and Tamika knew she was still using.

"Girl did you hear about Aliza who dance down at Magic City?"

"No!" Tamika replied.

"Girl, Aliza and about a dozen other bitches had a pumping party."

Tamika was in a fog. "A what kind of party?"

"A pumping party."

"What's that?"

"That's when they come out and inject silicone into their butts and hips for a curvaceous figure. Big round asses are believed to make more money."

"Stop playing."

"Girl, I ain't playing with you."

"How much does something like that cost?"

"They were charging eight hundred per girl."

"Damn, that's a come up at one party."

"Well, that's not even half the story yet. Why did the silicone travel through her body and into her arteries killing her early this morning?"

"Stop playing."

"Girl, I don't play like that!"

"Oh my God!"

"Three of the other girls have developed infections in their bloodstreams and they are asking the other nine girls to come forward. It was all over Fox News most of the day."

"Wow, that's crazy Princess."

"The couple that was administering the shots is on the run now. The news report said that they are going to be charged with murder."

"Damn, that's some serious shit."

"Yeah, you telling me! So Tamika when are we going to hang out!"

The question stunted Tamika who had no intention of ever opening herself up to that world again. She decided to be diplomatic about her answer. "Princess I'll love to hang out but I'm on my hustle right now."

Princess did not like that answer at all. Who was this bitch to snob her? She was a veteran in this game. This little fresh turnout was not going to act cute with her. *What she think, because she got a condo downtown and a ride, she's better than me? I'll fix that ass.* She was very coy in her approach. "Hey Tamika, what are you doing later on about eleven o'clock?"

"I don't have any plans. Hopefully I'll be on a call making some money. Why do you ask?"

"Well I got this client off of Metropolitan and Joseph E. Lowery Boulevard. You know the Metropolis Lofts on the corner?"

"Yeah, I know where that is."

"He asked me if I had a girl that he'll like and I know for a fact you're just his type."

"Princess I don't know about that. Nigga's over on that end don't have no money to be tricking off."

"Girl he's a dope boy, with plenty of paper."

"Well, why don't you just go see him?"

"He said he wanted to see someone new. You know these niggas be wanting variety."

"I don't know, I really don't be taking calls outside of the agency."

"Bitch are you dumb? Why would you want to continue giving Czar and them at the office a percentage of your money that you done fucked for? I'm not asking you to break me off anything Tamika!"

"How much is he paying?"

A smile curled on Princess's lips before she answered. "Two hundred and fifty dollars!"

"Okay Princess, text me his name and number I'll give him a call."

"I surely will Tamika." The ladies hung up.

After hanging up, Princess whispered the words, "Got you!"

Two minutes later Tamika's phone alerted her of an incoming text. It read, "Terrell" followed by a phone number. Tamika replied back to the text, "Got it."

Tamika called Beverly next. "Hey sis, what's happening!"

"I just got out of class. What have you been up too?"

"I'm on the way home from a call. Did you hear about Aliza and those other girls getting butt injections?"

"How could I not hear about it? The news has been looping it all day long."

"That's so, so sad. I wonder what's going to happen with her five year old son."

"I think she's from North Carolina so they'll just send him to live with her folks up there. Tamika, when is the next time we could get together? I really need to vent and get your opinion."

"When did I become an authority on love and relationships?" Tamika asked laughing. "Do you know I've never been in a healthy relationship in my life?"

"I just need you to listen to me little sis."

"I know I was just teasing you."

"Between Donavan pouring his heart out and Jonathan pouring his money out, I'm between a rock and a hard place."

"I wonder which one is the hard place," Tamika joked, grinning at her own comment.

"Stop it Tamika, I'm being very serious. Donavan still has not tried to pressure me to sleep with him. And the more he doesn't, the more I want to. It's weird, huh?"

"I tell you what Beverly, let's have lunch tomorrow on me. The weather is supposed to be really nice. We'll find a spot with a patio and work this out for you."

"That's what I'm talking about little sis."

"I have a movie date with Donavan tonight so I'll call you in the morning and we'll make plans."

"Cool."

After hanging up, Tamika dialed my number. I got the call while I was entertaining a sexy chocolate vixen who had absolutely nothing to do with the service. Dealing with square chicks outside of the industry gave me a sense of normalcy. I answered the phone on the third ring, finishing my thought to my guest before saying, "Hello."

"What up Czar."

"Hey Tamika, what's up with you?"

"Just hollering at you."

"Hold on one second, Tamika."

"OKAY!"

I suggested Mexican food to my passenger and she giggled in agreement. "Okay, I'm back."

"Well, don't let me bother you if you have company."

"Nah, it's cool. We can talk. I hear you've been on a mission. When I went in the other morning and was looking at the logged calls on the computer, you were down for more calls than any other girl at the agency."

"Yeah Czar, I'm trying to formulate an exit plan."

Before I could answer, my female passenger asked something in the background.

Tamika heard this and immediately thought of it as simplistic shit from an insecure girl. This girl didn't want shit but to have her presence known to whomever was on the other end of the phone call. She knew how those hoes operated. "Look Czar, I can hit you back later to catch up." She could tell she did not have my undivided attention by the delay in my answers.

"Uh, yeah Tamika that will work. Hit me tomorrow or something."

And with that the conversation was over. Tamika was nowhere on my radar–at least nowhere that I would admit to. After cutting the phone call with Tamika short, I felt guilty she was reaching out to me for a reason and I did not offer her the attention she was seeking.

Tamika decided to call the office to see if any calls were coming in. Tee picked up the phone.

"Hey Tee, I was just checking to see if you had a call for me?"

"Nah girl, it's been a bit slow today."

"Okay hit me up if something come through."

"I will Tamika."

Tamika looked at the text message she had received from Princess earlier that day, which read "Terrell." Every fiber in her body and spirit told her that it was a bad idea to make the call but she went against her better judgment. She dialed Terrell's number with much apprehension. Maybe he would not even answer the phone she thought. No such luck, Terrell answered right away.

"Who dis?" was the way he answered the phone—turn off number one.

"This is Tamika, Princess's friend."

"Oh yeah, she said you'll be calling. What took you so long? I thought you didn't want this money."

Changing the subject, Tamika replied, "So, what time did you want me to come over?"

"Hold on Miss Lady, can you describe yourself for me?"

"Well, I'm five-foot-eight, one hundred forty-pounds, 34C-32-36, nice and toned, no stretch marks or scars on my body."

"Damn, that sounds good. What celebrity would you say you look like?"

"What?" He asked the silly-ass question again.

"I've been told that with my hair short I look like Halle Berry."

"Stop playing girl."

"I'm not playing. I'm sure you'll be happy with my appearance and more pleased with my performance."

"Can you get here in about two hours? I have a quick run to make."

"Yeah I can."

Terrell gave her the gate code and the unit number and then asked if she would wear some heels.

"I certainly will." Tamika looked at her watch, it was eight o'clock. "So, I'll see you at ten o'clock."

Terrell agreed on the time then hung up. Tamika knew it would only take her ten to fifteen minutes to get to his spot; it was a straight shot down Northside Drive from her place. She also decided to wear what she had on. This nigga would not be able to appreciate the extra effort that she put in for her Buckhead clients. Two hours came fast and she was en route to meet Terrell. The butterflies in the pit of her stomach were telling her to call Beverly and at least let her know where she would be. The thought of interrupting her date with Donavan killed that idea. Calling me would just put her on buggaboo status with me, not to mention, she did not need confirmation that I was still out with that other chick. Tamika composed herself and deduced that she was not far from home. She would knock this call out and be back home by eleven-twenty.

Tamika pulled up to the gatepad of Terrell's complex and entered the four digits he had given her earlier. Like magic, the gate retracted to let her in. Tamika pulled around to his unit where a white Escalade was parked on twenty-four-inch rims, no doubt Terrell's truck. She just shook her head and thought, *typical nigga.* She knocked on the door and a hulking six-foot-two figure greeted her. His mouth was gleaming from the gold grill that replaced his teeth—both on the top and at the bottom.

"Damn shorty, you right on time. I like that. I like that!"

Tamika reluctantly stepped inside. The aroma of weed and alcohol stained the air of his place. Her eyes darted around the room taking in everything all at once. He had all the tricks of his trade in open view for all to see—individual bags of weed and crack packages for sale, a bunch of loose small bills scattered about and a .357 revolver on the kitchen counter. *This fool don't know me well enough to have all this shit out here like this,* she thought.

Her gaze returned to Terrell, as he said, "What you looking around like that for? We the only ones here. You good little Mama, don't be acting so scary." Tamika forced a smile to make herself seem more comfortable than she really was. She was still clutching onto her purse which hung on her shoulder. "That's it little Mama, put a smile on that pretty face of yours."

Looking at his six-two frame, Terrell was not a bad-looking guy. He was medium-brown complexion, about two hundred and thirty pounds and he wore his hair braided back. Anyone could tell he worked out regularly and, from his numerous tattoos, he had spent some time in the penal system. Jail tattoos always showed themselves from lack of adequate tools in the joint.

Tamika decided she would do a fake check-in to put Terrell on notice that someone knew where she was. "Hey, this is Tamika checking in. Okay! I'll call you when I'm checking out, bye." Tamika was actually talking to her own voicemail.

Terrell looked up from the corner of his eyes, observing and listening to Tamika. The white wife-beater that he had on was form-fitting, hugging his biceps and V-shaped torso. A little too thugged-out for Tamika's taste but he was definitely good-looking. "You want something to smoke or drink? I got some of this Diddy juice." He held up an open bottle of Ciroc.

Tamika quietly answered, "No, thank you."

"Shit, what was I thinking? You're a friend of Princess. You want some of that powder right?"

"Nah, I don't do coke either!" This was the first time Tamika had been around any cocaine since quitting cold-turkey some months prior. She could feel the anxiety build up in her. The thought of the drugs in her body gave her a warm comforting feeling. All addicts, even if they never used again in their lives, would always be addicted physiologically. Her mind started to question, *what would one or two lines of coke hurt?* Temptation and the high that she knew was only three letters away—Y-E-S!

Terrell was now crushing some cocaine up in a folded bill standing directly in front of Tamika. He sniffed a line that he meticulously created on the glass table in front of them. Then he looked up at Tamika, saying, "The offer still stands little Mama," as he stretched out a line for her. Tamika thought of all she had accomplished—her own condo, nice car, regained weight and self-esteem. She reflected most of all on the life she watched her own mother live as a drug addict. No, she was going to be the first in her family to attend college. She was not about to throw it all away. She was frustrated now!

"Look Terrell, I did not come over here for that."

"Princess did say you were a bourgeoi, stuck-up bitch." Terrell stood up and towered over her as she remained sitting. "Look bitch, you cute and all but you don't have to be acting like that."

Tamika started to eye the locked door on the other side of the room. Terrell was on her, in her face talking loud. She could see the effect of the drug taking precedence over him as he was becoming more volatile.

"Take your clothes off bitch. Let me see that pretty pussy."

At this point Tamika knew she had to play it cool to get out of there. "Can I go and get undressed in the bathroom?"

"Do you think I'm stupid or something?" Tamika attempted to stand up, but Terrell's massive body was not going to allow that. He started staring away at the blouse she had on, suddenly yanking the front of it. The buttons came off in sequence, one after the other and landed on the floor, exposing her. "Those some nice fucking breasts you got."

Tamika started to recollect the previous ordeal of being raped when she was younger. She was now a different person in a different time. She yelled for help as loud as she could. He quieted her with an open hand slap across her face. The blow made Tamika see stars and created a ringing sound in her ears. Her hand was fumbling with the zipper of her purse. Terrell had not noticed that Tamika's right hand was searching around in her bag for something. He got off of her momentarily to pull his own pants down to his ankles. It was enough time for Tamika to grab hold of the orange box cutter that she concealed in her bag. She eased the blade out of its position with her thumb, while still inside of the bag. Terrell's erect penis was waving up and down like a diving board plank. It took everything bit of self-control for Tamika not to wave the blade onto his dick. She knew that she had only one shot at getting out of there and she could not blow it. She had to strike hard and fierce or he would surely kill her.

She knew she could not run in her four-inch Christian Louboutin red bottom shoes. She used her left foot to kick off the right shoe and the right foot to kick off the left shoe. When Terrell saw this he thought that she was helping him undress herself. "That's what I'm talking about. You're going to enjoy this babe, I promise." He got down on his knees to pull off her stockings. She was now face-to-face on the same level as Terrell. That would be his one and only mistake.

He pulled the stockings down to her knees and looked up to say something. That's when Tamika's right hand appeared with the box cutter, slashing Terrell from right to left across his face. Tamika was initially surprised by her own precision and the sight of blood squirting from Terrell's face. She had opened him up well and good with a six-inch track. She saw the white of his flesh before it became engulfed in crimson. It was at that very moment every bit of rage that Tamika had felt in her life was about to be released onto Terrell.

Terrell was clutching his face with both hands and screaming, "Bitch, I'm going to kill you!"

His hands were over his face and his sight was partially skewed by blood, leaving his chest wide open. Tamika though about her mother's boyfriend taking her virginity, then slashed at his chest. She thought about her father abandoning her, then slashed at his arms. She thought about her mother's addiction to crack, then slashed at his throat. Terrell's formerly white wife-beater was now beet red, soaked in his own blood. Tamika was yelling at the top of her voice. "Who's the bitch now? Who's the bitch now?!"

As if she really wanted an answer, Tamika reached for the open bottle of Ciroc Vodka and doused Terrell's cuts with the alcohol. Terrell wailed in pain, his long arms managing to back slap Tamika to the ground, smearing his blood all over her. He was not interested in fighting with her as long as she had that blade in her hand. He pushed past her, heading for the kitchen counter, where the .357 revolver laid in wait for his hands. She knew exactly where and for what he was heading.

Tamika scampered to her feet and jetted toward the locked front door. She knew that he would reach the gun before she could unlock the door. The sound of the hammer cocking back confirmed it. Terrell had the gun in hand, aimed at her back. At that very moment Tamika asked God to forgive her of any sins that she had committed against His word. Tamika heard the loud roar of the high power handgun and waited to feel its impact. She felt the velocity of the bullet whiz past her right shoulder and crash through the door. Either Terrell was a bad shot or God had interceded! Tamika's heart was beating wildly with fear. Fumbling with the lock and the doorknob, she managed to swing the door open. Terrell, frustrated with blood in his eyes, squeezed off the remaining four shots in no particular direction, just out of anger. Bullets traveled through the thin walls into other units. One went through the ceiling to the upstairs neighbor's place. You could hear the clicking of the hammer way after he had spent his five rounds.

Tamika ran outside into the night air partially naked. A small crowd of five residents had formed a few doors down. One of the older gentlemen took off his jacket and draped it over Tamika's shirtless body. He held her close and said, "It's okay, the police are on their way. We knew one day that that boy was going to kill someone. He ain't been nothing but trouble since he got here. We were tired of his loud music and his thug friends."

Tamika stood there shivering as she heard sirens in the distance getting closer and closer, no doubt on their way there. Police swarmed the area and rushed into Terrell's loft, finding him passed out on the floor, gun still in hand. He had so much blood loss that he collapsed and blacked out on the floor. The police were shocked to see that this was the same Terrell that had been implicated in a murder that took place a few months earlier off of Candler Road in Decatur. The gun that was used was also a .357, no doubt the same weapon that was used in the homicide.

After a female officer interviewed Tamika, it was determined that she had to be arrested on assault charges. It was only as a formality since they were certain that she was just defending herself. Tamika was also possibly eligible for the ten thousand dollar reward, since Terrell was one of Georgia's Most Wanted and she in fact did capture him. They brought the still unconscious Terrell out on a stretcher, handcuffed to the rails. He was hooked up to an I.V. drip. Between the murder charge and all the drugs they found in his place, Terrell would never see the light of day again. The police took the bloodied orange box cutter and placed it into a plastic bag marked "Evidence."

The cop processing the evidence yelled over to his Sergeant, "Are we going to charge her for having a weapon?"

The Sergeant looked over at Tamika now sitting in the back of the marked patrol car's backseat in handcuffs. He responded, "That little lady has beeen through enough tonight. She's lucky to be alive. That dude is a cold-blooded killer. It's best that she got caught with it than to get caught without it." With that said, he jumped into his own squad car and left.

Princess knew Terrell's M.O. was to get girls over there and get them high and fuck them for free all night. She did not bank on Tamika turning down the drugs and wanting her money. Princess did not envy Tamika because she was making more money than her or the fact that she had gotten her own condo downtown. Nor was it her new luxury car. She hated Tamika because she watched Tamika clean up her act and started looking for an out in a life that she felt that she was eternally trapped in herself—the old crabs in a barrel attitude. A lot of these girls felt like there was nothing else they could do besides sell their bodies.

# 10
# EXIT PLAN

"A farewell is necessary before we could meet again."

Standing there on Tamika's balcony made me realize how much I wanted out of this industry; just as much as most of the girls that lived it did. If Tamika would have been murdered by Terrell I don't know how I would have handled it. I saw her for who she was from the first day that we met, despite the hard persona that she put on.

It was still pretty early in the morning so I opted not to call Beverly and wake her up with bad news. Tamika had gotten out of her warm bath and into her own bed and was fast asleep. I contemplated leaving but I did not want Tamika to wake up and panic when she realized that I was gone. She was still very much shaken up over the events of the night. I looked in on her sleeping like the baby that she truly was then I walked into her guest bedroom and went to sleep myself.

I decided to wake up very early the following morning and get the day off with a nice breakfast. I put the breakfast menu together mentally while I looked through Tamika's refrigerator. *Okay! I can make some shrimp and cheese scrambled eggs with grits, turkey bacon and some fresh fruit on the side.* I wondered if Tamika drank hot chocolate or coffee with her breakfast. I decided to peek into her room. She was still very much asleep. I could hear my phone vibrating on the kitchen counter from an incoming call. Who could be calling me this early? I picked up my phone and saw the name, "Beverly" on its display.

"Hey, good morning Beverly."

"Good morning my ass. Where's Tamika?" There was a sincere conviction coupled with genuine concern in her voice.

It warmed my heart and brought a smile to my face to see how close these two strangers had become. "She's fine Beverly, she's asleep right now. I was about to fix her some breakfast. How did you hear about what happened?"

"Everyone is talking about that lunatic Terrell. You know these hoes run their mouth's like water. It was also posted up on the message board as well. The word is that Princess set Tamika up for that bullshit."

"Yeah, is that so! I really had not gotten a chance to ask Tamika any details about the situation. "Hey Beverly, why don't you get dressed and come have breakfast with us. It will be ready in thirty minutes. Is that enough time for you to get over here? You're only a few blocks."

"Okay, I'll throw on something really fast."

"Cool, see you in a few."

I began making my famous cheese eggs and shrimps that were usually reserved for one of my special overnight guests. I felt like Tamika was more than deserving, especially after the traumatic night she just experienced. It must have been a combination of the sizzling bacon and the aroma that woke Tamika up. Tamika stumbled out of her room, still rubbing her eyes in an attempt to be fully awake herself. She had on a t-shirt and panties. I looked up from what I was doing to stare for a moment. Damn, even her morning face looked good.

She flashed a smile at me from where she was standing, as if to say thank you. I nodded in understanding to her. I broke the quiet of the morning.

"How do you feel?"

She paused and gestured her hand over to what I was doing and said, "I feel so, so blessed, Czar." I could see the water welling up in her eyes already. She took three quick steps before she was in my arms. She did not want me to see her get all emotional so she held her face over my shoulder. "Terrell could have killed me last night."

I think the reality had hit her for the first time. I responded. "But he didn't, it was not your time."

Tamika dried her eyes and fixed herself then asked, "Where is the hot chocolate?"

Smiling to myself, I knew the little girl in her was more of a hot chocolate type than coffee. "Oh, Beverly is on her way over to have breakfast with us, as well."

"Do she know what happened last night?"

"Yeah, it seems like everyone knows the details but me Tamika."

Tamika stopped and held one hand over her head and the other on her waist as she shook her head. The garage intercom was integrated to the phone system for entry. When Tamika's phone rang she asked, "Who is it?"

"It's Beverly!"

Tamika pressed the five button to let her in the gate. Two minutes later, Beverly was knocking on the door. I opened the door without asking who it was. Beverly rushed past me without one word and into Tamika's arms. Beverly bear-hugged Tamika for a solid three minutes in a rocking motion, tears streaming down her face. She then abruptly released her grips of Tamika and her tone turned to anger.

"Why didn't you tell me or Czar you were going on a call?"

Tamika, glanced up at me, stuttering her words. "Czar, Czar was out with some chick… and you were with Donavan. I did not want to interrupt what ya'll had going on with my bullshit."

Beverly's tone had now softened. "Sis, we are a team. I'll always be there for you."

I confirmed that I felt the same way with a head nod that was met with a smile from Tamika. After we all exchanged embraces acknowledging our newfound understanding, we sat down to have breakfast together. I decided that I would bless the meal. "God, thank You for this meal we are about to receive. Thank You for protecting our sister with Your grace and mercy, delivering her from the den of death and suffering. We pray for guidance, diligence and patience in steering us through a different path in life. Amen."

I could hear both women conclude with stern, "AMENS." They said it with such conviction, it was as if it was so already. I did not want the breakfast conversation to be dominated with the events of the past night so I decided to probe Beverly about her date last night.

"Hey Beverly, how's the yard man, Donavan doing?"

As if I had caught her totally off guard with that question, she took a long pause, held her head over her plate and started playing with the food on her plate with the fork.

"Did you hear me?"

She looked up with the biggest telltale smile that was so obvious. Before she could muster any sort of reply, Tamika blurted out, "YOU FUCKED HIM, DIDN'T YOU!"

Beverly started blushing and turning colors in her face.

"Good for you sis," Tamika followed up.

"I feel so bad knowing that I was screwing and you were fighting for your life."

Tamika eased her guilt, "You did not put me there nor did you have anything to do with it Beverly! Let's place the blame where it belongs, on Terrell."

I jumped in again shifting gears, "So you really like him, huh?"

"I do Czar."

"Do you think you're in love with him?"

Without missing a beat, she answered, "Yes." You could see the glee in Beverly's face as well as the happiness that Tamika felt for her.

Tamika reached for Beverly's hand and said, "I hope to find that one day."

I started feeling really warm as Tamika delivered that line accompanied with a gaze in my direction. After a bit of an uncomfortable silence, Beverly's voice pierced the air. "I've had boyfriends in the past but I think I made love for the very first time last night."

I heard all kinds of "Ooh's" and "Aww's" coming from Tamika.

Then a peculiar thing happened. Beverly's blissful attitude was suddenly saddened.

Tamika picked up on it as well and asked, "What's wrong Bev?"

"I just can't go on deceiving Donavan like this."

"I understand sis!"

"He told me how special I was to him and how proud he was of me as far as school and all that. As he was telling me all these great things about myself, all I could think of was how much it would hurt him if he knew about me escorting, selling my body. I'll be graduating in a couple of weeks. I have to make a clean break once and for all."

Then she turned to me and asked, "Czar do you think it's a good or bad idea to ever share my past escorting with Donavan in the future."

"Well Beverly, I get asked that question a lot by girls who get into relationships after escorting. And I must admit, it's not a clear-cut answer. I totally believe in complete honesty in a relationship, let me start by saying that. Whether or not to be candid about your past as an escort really depends on what kind of man you're dealing with. In one aspect, you could forge a stronger trust being vulnerable in that way and trusting that you won't be judged. Take me for example. I'm not a square guy and I'm not possessive. I may be a lot more objective in receiving that sort of news from someone I'm going out with. Then you have a different type of dude that the first argument that you guys have you'll be a million whores, bitches and some more shit. So you see it's not as simple as black and white. You know him better than I do, so I won't be able to answer that in your case. Now if you want an across the board answer as to tell him or not to tell him about your escorting past I would say, NO, don't say a damn thing."

I could visibly see a sense of relief come over Beverly. No doubt that information was now going into the secret vault that most women had. Tamika was such an opportunist and I should have seen it coming, knowing how witty she was. "Okay Czar, are you saying that you would be open to having a relationship with a woman that you knew was a hoe, excuse me, an escort?" The smirk on her face was very suggestive.

I composed myself and took a deep breath before answering her. "Tamika, I have a past as well. The best thing about that is that I am not the same person I was yesterday. So, if I would not want to be judged by who I was when I was younger, I won't judge anyone solely on their past challenges either."

The smirk was now gone from Tamika's face. I guess my answer was not to her liking. "Why you have to always be all politically correct and shit? Let me put this really simple for you Czar. How would you feel knowing that your girlfriend or wife fucked a bunch of random men for money? Could you ever really respect her? Would you ever really love her? What's that shit all you men always saying? You can't turn a hoe into a housewife."

I could tell that Tamika was really questioning her own morality and her conscience was eating at her. Most of these girls knew that they were bigger and better than the decisions that they made to escort. I guess from the outside it looked glamorous and easy. What they did not account for was the emotional and psychological price that came with it.

Tamika was relentless. She continued to egg me on. "Or you can fuck a hoe but you won't take her home to Mama type deal."

I jumped in. "I think I already gave you a sufficient answer Tamika."

She continued on. "Okay, let me ask you this question. What makes me different from a woman that marries a man for his money?" It was really a rhetorical question because Tamika was giving me her perspective before I could even share my thoughts. "Well let me tell you, the difference is that I'm up front and honest about the nature of the relationship. A bitch that takes vows in front of God knowing that it's a lie in her heart is no better than I am."

Beverly who had been sitting silent watching the exchange between us, saw that her sister was internalizing the hurt of the conversation on the table and jumped in. "Tamika, you're a beautiful girl on the inside and out. If a man don't want you based on what you did in the past, well, that's his loss." Beverly went on edifying Tamika between forks full of food. "You're smart and strong. Look how far you've come in just a few months of us meeting."

Beverly's last statement cemented her objective. Tamika's esteem came back and she reflected on how she saw the world before and now. It had been such a narrow existence but now she had greater goals than she could ever imagine. The last thing I wanted to do was to make Tamika feel inadequate but in the same breathe, she couldn't project her guilt of her actions onto me either. I wanted to ease the tension so I got up and walked over to where Tamika sat and hugged her. I squeezed her in my arms and said, "Any man would be happy to have someone so persistent as you."

I could feel her return the squeezing as she pressed her midsection up against mine. Beverly's sighs and, "Mmm, huhs!" broke up our play time. "Why don't you two just do it and get it over with. I can feel the sexual tension between you two."

Neither Tamika nor I would confirm or deny Beverly's words. Our eyes locked into a stare and they told the truth. Breakfast was certainly over now. We all cleared our plates from the table and adjourned to the living room with its floor-to-ceiling sliding door that led out onto the patio. It was clear that we all needed to regroup and really start thinking of this exit plan.

I started with Tamika first. "So what are you going to do now Tamika?"

"What do you mean, what am I going to do now? Ain't shit changed. I'm going to relax for the next few days and pamper myself then I'm going to call on and let the office know I'm available. That's what I'm going to do Czar. That buster Terrell did not slow down my hustle one bit. His ass is laid up in the hospital cut the fuck up and is about to spend the rest of his life in a fucking jail cell. And when I catch up with that bitch Princess I'm going to blow her from ear to ear. Buck fifty that hoe for hating on me like that." Tamika said that with a devilish smile and a lot of emotion in her voice. "Czar I'm going to need another box cutter by the way."

Beverly and I busted out laughing at her humor about the whole situation.

"Princess's phone is off and no one has been able to get in touch with her," Beverly said.

"Maybe she took her ass back to New York! I should really be thanking her to tell you the truth."

A question mark was on both Beverly's and my face.

Tamika continued. "The investigating officer told me that I was eligible to receive the ten thousand dollar reward they had for Terrell's capture."

"You certainly did capture that nigga too girl," Beverly responded. "I mean what is your long term plan Tamika?"

"Well, I'm going to apply for fall admission at Spelman or Clark and follow in the steps of my big sister. I'm going to major in communications and possibly parlay a career in media when I graduate."

"I can really see you in front of the camera or on the radio with all that personality that you got."

"Thank you Czar!"

"Well, you've done everything that you said you'll do so far. I have no doubt that you'll succeed there too. I think that's a great exit plan Tamika."

Our attention shifted to Beverly simultaneously and without saying a word she understood it was her turn. "Well, as you both know, I'm about to graduate in a few more weeks. With a economics degree in hand I hope to land a job that would give me the experience to eventually start my own business. What I'm looking forward to most of all is to have real structure back in my life, like the kind I grew up knowing between my mom and dad. I have a really good feeling about Donavan, you guys have no idea. He's very excited about meeting my mother when she comes down for the graduation. Czar, do you remember the advice that you gave me in reference to meeting the man I'd like to marry?"

"I've given you too much dating advice to remember all."

"Well, this one is where you told me in order to be someone's wife I should start playing the role of a wife. Well, tomorrow night I'm going to cook Donavan dinner. I'm going the old school approach through his stomach." You could hear laughter throughout the living room at Beverly's old school tactics.

"You know that might just work Beverly."

Tamika then chimed in. "Is that what I have to do to get your attention Czar, cook for you?"

"Well, I love to eat."

"That's what I keep hearing but have yet to experience it." Tamika's witty and slick mouth never vacationed at all.

"I really wish that you guys would fuck and just get it over with already," Beverly said.

Tamika raised her eyebrows as if to say, "Well, I'm game."

Beverly continued talking, "I'm going to make Donavan the happiest man on earth. You guys need to be around when he calls me his "Yankee Queen." His accent and the look on his face are priceless."

Tamika was forever with the jokes. "I hope he's not just trying to get his green card."

Laughter erupted once again. "He's already a United States citizen excuse you!"

"No, no I'm just teasing," Tamika playfully told Beverly.

"I have just one loose end to tie up."

Tamika and I waited to hear what that loose end was. Beverly took a deep breath and said, "JONATHAN. I did not want to worry you guys but I think Jonathan has been stalking my complex and spying on me."

"How so?"

"Well, I thought I saw his car in my complex then he called my phone and asked what was I doing and where I was. I think more so to see if I would lie to him or not. He's become way more demanding over the last few weeks. The line is really blurred for him. He don't see this as a client-escort relationship anymore. He really thinks I'm like his girlfriend. The more I pull away, the more he does for me. He's been paying my rent and lavishing me with jewelry that I could care less about."

"Would that beautiful tennis bracelet on your arm be a piece of the jewelry that you could care less about?" Tamika asked, reaching for Beverly's wrist.

"Yes it is!" She took it off to show Tamika.

Tamika held the bracelet up to the sun, the brilliant prisms reflected back a spectrum of dazzling color. "Ooh girl, look at that. Those have to be VVS diamonds up in there, look at how it gleams."

Tamika clasped the bracelet around her own wrist and began admiring it. Beverly looked at it on Tamika's hand and said, "It looks good on you sis."

"Thank you." Tamika took it off and reached to hand it back to Beverly.

Beverly never reached back for it. "I want you to have it Tamika!"

"What! I can't accept it Bev, it's yours."

"Please take it as a token of our sisterhood. The other day Donavan and I were walking in the park. He stopped and picked a nearby flower and placed it in my hair while onlookers just stared. That flower and this bracelet don't have the same value to me sis so please accept it."

She did not have to twist Tamika's arm too much harder. "Thank you Bev." She reached over to hug and kiss her on the cheek. "Wow, this is the nicest gift I've ever gotten in my life sis."

I sat back in awe of the authentic love they had for one another.

"Czar, how do you think I should handle this situation with Jonathan?"

"I think you need to be very direct and blunt. Tackle it head on. Let him know that you're seeing someone and you're going to change your lifestyle."

"You don't understand Czar. He's not the type of guy to take no easily."

"If all else fails, I'll pick up the phone and make a man-to-man call to him myself.

"Ooh, would you do that for me as a last resort?!"

"Yeah, I got you Beverly."

"The last thing I want is Donavan finding out and getting involved in any way."

"That's the least of your worries Beverly. It will all work out."

"I believe you Czar! Well, you've heard my plans and Tamika's plans. What's yours?"

"You girls don't want to hear my plans. It's not as exciting as yours."

"Oh yes we do!"

"Whether you girls know it or not, I want a change of lifestyle just as much as you two do. I may not be an escort but think about the weird hours and the dysfunctional relationships I've fostered. I guess as I mature, my views sort of change. No offense but I don't want to be surrounded by hoes much longer. I'm really tired of hiding what I do from everyone that I come into contact with. My family has no idea about this part of my life. I don't know what they think I do. I mean whenever I meet a decent female I dread the, 'What do you do?' conversation. I usually answer with a broad, vague response like, 'I'm in personnel management' which is the truth, right?"

The two of them got such a kick out of my terminology, that Tamika came up with her own job title as a, "spousal hospitality administrator."

"That's a creative and very accurate job description too, Mama."

After we all laughed at Tamika's clever word play, I got back to the more serious topic of what was my exit plan was. "To be honest with ya'll, I've already started on working on my exit plan."

"Well, don't keep us in suspense. What is it that you're going to do?"

"I'm going to start a luxury car service. I just got my chauffeur's license back in the mail. The next move is to go downtown and get my business license. Since Atlanta Hartsfield Jackson is the busiest airport in the world now, a lot of my clients will be business travelers. I'll need to get my airport permit on my cars and an airport badge. I already spoke with a car dealer about financing two other cars. The next step would be to find reliable professional drivers that I could trust and depend on."

"Damn Czar, I'm really liking that idea a whole lot."

"Thank you Beverly! When we get up and running maybe you could come aboard to dispatch drivers and run the day-to-day office operations."

"I would more than love too Czar!"

Tamika's face was solemn but not out of fear or anger. "This is the first time I've ever been around such progressive people such as ya'll. I mean with all this talk and planning I really see an out for the first time in my life. You two have given me hope!"

"Thank you for saying that, Tamika."

"No, it's true Beverly."

Beverly went on as if she had an afterthought. "I want you guys to formally meet Donavan before graduation. I was thinking lunch or dinner. I did not want everyone meeting for the very first time at graduation, with my moms flying in and all! Ya'll not going to believe that Jonathan really thought that I was going to invite him to my graduation. I have to break it off with him before that. He hinted that he wanted to do something really nice for me since this is such a 'big step in my life' as he puts it."

"Yeah Beverly, I'm not feeling good about Jonathan at all."

"I don't think he'll be that big of a problem, Czar. Shit, this is him calling me right now. We done talked him up."

Beverly held up her index finger in the air to excuse herself as she walked away for privacy. I continued talking with Tamika but I was transfixed on Beverly's phone conversation. Even though I could not hear one word through the sliding glass balcony door, I could read her body language as her flaring arms went up and down. I sensed that Jonathan Weilz was going to be a lot more trouble than Beverly could foresee.

"Czar, why you being so nosy?" Tamika observed me clocking Beverly's reaction to Jonathan on the phone.

"I'm not being nosy. Someone has to look out for you two."

"Yeah, I know Czar. I know."

Beverly abruptly ended her call and stormed back inside from the balcony. She was obviously upset but did not want to talk. She just started to gather her things and said that she was leaving. Her phone rang again while still in her hand. She looked at the screen then immediately sent it to her voicemail after shaking her head. She repeated this action a half dozen times consecutively.

I could not just sit there and say nothing. "Beverly where are you going?"

She turned to me in a Shakespearian voice and said, "A farewell is necessary before we could meet again."

I decided to entertain her. "When shall we meet again?" I asked in my best Shakespearian effort.

She came out of character and said, "Let's meet with Donavan tomorrow for an early dinner; maybe around sixish?" She looked at me for confirmation on the time.

"Yeah, six o'clock would work for me."

Beverly then looked towards Tamika. She agreed that six o'clock was cool as well. We all exchanged hugs before Beverly walked out the door saying, "See you guys tomorrow."

Her phone rang once more, changing the look on her face to a grimace as she repeated the action of sending the call to her voicemail once again.

After Beverly left, I realized that I had spent the better part of the day at Tamika's condo. I decided to break out as well. "Tamika, I'm about to leave."

"Oh I see, me and you together alone and you want to run off, huh Czar!"

"You know I have to take care of business. I can't sit around here all day Mama."

"Well, it's not going to be that easy to leave."

"Really?"

Tamika got right up in my face, very suggestively. "I'm not going to let you walk out of here without sharing one of your poems with me."

I relaxed, knowing that I could meet her demand without much effort. "Okay, that's not a problem Tamika. I have something very appropriate. Since Beverly is in love and you are in lust, I have a joint called Love vs. Lust."

Tamika teasingly placed her index finger in her mouth and squinted her eyes flirtatiously at me. I smiled at her and began reciting Love vs. Lust.

Love vs. Lust

Love and Lust are identical twins; carried for nine months by mother Universe.

Lust always envied Love for being born first. Sometimes Lust dresses up like Love to

Fool us.

Lust hated to see Love grow.

Love is words; Lust is touch.

Love seeks the heart; Lust seeks the flesh.

Love is monogamous; Lust is promiscuous.

Love is slow; Lust is fast.

Love is a phone call; Lust is a text.

Love is forgiving; Lust holds a grudge.

Love is honest; Lust lies.

Lust mimics Love, veiled in similarity exposed only by true emotion. Love smiles, caresses and comforts. Lust deceives, confuses and hurts.

In the end, Love will flourish.

By, Ceasar Mason

When I was finished, Tamika did a single person applause for me. She clapped her hands excitedly for a full two minutes.

"Where do you come up with this stuff Czar?"

"From life's experiences, to tell you the truth."

Tamika put her arms around me to hug me with appreciation. It was not in a lustful way. I think I was getting through to her now. "Czar I can really see the contrast between love and lust. You illustrate such vivid images through your words. It's easy for a woman's emotions to misinterpret lust for love." Tamika thanked me again for sharing my poetry and mentioned how much she looked forward to meeting Donavan at dinner the following day.

The following day we ultimately decided to eat at Papadeaux on Jimmy Carter. Tamika and I drove together with me opting to ride in her car. I decided to park my whip in her parking garage. I had spent numerous days driving her from call to call. It was a breath of fresh air to be in her passenger seat now. It was a beautiful Atlanta day. Tamika had the top down on her convertible. I just watched her as she weaved in and out of traffic, bobbing her head to the music on the radio. I was just in awe of this young lady and her resilience. I smiled at how much of a difference a day makes. She was in a life or death situation just a day ago. WOW, talk about bouncing back!

We pulled into the parking lot ten minutes early. Beverly and Donavan had not arrived yet. Tamika and I walked in and were greeted by the hostess. She was a slender white chick in her mid-twenties, possibly working her way through school. Her name tag read Becky.

"Welcome to Papadeaux, how many in your party today?"

I spoke before Tamika could answer. "It will be four of us and a booth would be fine."

"What's the name?"

"It's Mason!"

"Okay Mr. Mason, you'll be seated in five minutes."

"Okay, thanks Becky."

"You guys do have the option to sit at the bar while you wait."

Tamika started to make a beeline towards the bar in lieu of the waiting area up in front. She took about three steps in the bar's direction with me in tow then she did a peculiar thing. She stopped cold in her tracks and turned back around towards the front again. I was following her, so I was baffled with her change of direction. Becky's facial expression kind of asked the same question.

Tamika picked up on Becky's concern and said, "On second thought, we'll just wait here for the rest of our dinner party."

That answer satisfied Becky's curiosity but not mine.

"Tamika what's going on with you?"

"Shh, for a second Czar."

"Shh, for what?"

"Don't look but that couple with the two kids to the left of the bar..."

Naturally, I turned my head to see who Tamika was referring to.

Tamika admonished me, "I said don't look."

"How else can I see who you're talking about Tamika?"

"Well, that guy is a regular client at the agency. I saw him two days ago."

"Damn!"

"Yeah, damn is right. I don't need to run into clients with their wife and kids. Czar look at his wife. She's beautiful."

"Yeah, she's fine as hell."

"I'm having a really low moment here!"

"Look Tamika, you didn't make him call our service."

"I know Czar, but my heart goes out to the son who looks about eight and his daughter that's about eleven."

At that very moment, the man looked up and saw Tamika. His wife's back was to us. Like most men in a situation like this, he fumbled. When he saw Tamika he froze up. Whatever his wife was asking went unanswered. He was like a deer in headlights, mouth open and all. It was his long stare across the room that also caught his wife's attention. We could see her peering over her own shoulders to see what had taken her husband's attention away from her. Tamika and I stood there not wanting to create waves in anyone's marriage. I could hear his wife ask from across the room, "Do you know those people?" still looking in our direction. What could he do but deny it! Tamika and I sat in the waiting area in silence. She seemed to be really shaken by seeing her client in his "real life."

She had a sense of victimizing his wife and kids I guess. Tamika kept her head down and avoided any eye contact in their direction. I knew she longed for that type of family life for herself so I guess she put herself in the wife's place. You know, what if the shoe was on the other foot sort of thing. Prostitution has longed been referred to as a victimless crime. I think we all were victims to a degree—the wife, kids and yes, even Tamika. The good thing was that we did not have to sit in condemnation for long. Beverly and Donavan walked through the restaurant door soon after.

"Hey you guys, sorry we're running a little later than expected."

I stood up to greet them both. "No Beverly, your timing is actually really good."

Beverly and Tamika exchanged cheek kisses hello. Beverly then poised herself and took a deep breath before introducing Donavan formally. "Czar, Tamika, I'd like you to meet Donavan."

Donavan's big broad smile went from ear to ear. He shook my hand with vigor and excitement. From his more formal attire I could tell he wanted to make a good impression on us.

Tamika greeted him with a hug and some kind words. "So you're the island man that has given my sister her groove back!"

We all laughed at the movie reference before being ushered to our booth on the other side of the restaurant. Donavan waited to sit after seeing the two ladies seated. A gentleman too, huh! I was not going to be outdone. I waited for him to sit as well before I took my own seat. Beverly was radiating in every way. She and Donavan really looked good together.

The waitress came and took our drink orders. Donavan was really attentive to Beverly's needs. He even ordered her drink knowing what she would want to have.

Tamika decided to jump right in and put Donavan in the hot seat. "So Donavan, tell us about yourself."

Donavan cleared his throat and in a mixture of an American and Jamaican accent, he began. Donavan started with his modest upbringing in the Tivoli Garden ghetto of Jamaica until his parents immigrated to the States. They first settled in Miami, Florida's Carol City section where he attended Carol City High School. He told a heart-breaking story that Beverly had obviously already heard, because her eyes started to water up before he even started to give any details of the story. Donavan was in love with his high school sweetheart with whom he had been engaged to be married. Unfortunately, she was one of the victims of a senseless drive-by shooting in which five people were shot, her being one of the three that would later die. Donavan felt it would be easier to get a fresh start in another state, hence his move to Georgia soon after.

You could hear and feel the sincerity and love in his tone as he shared his pain. Beverly reached over and clasped his hand within hers as a sign of support. I believe that they both related to the loss of a loved one with a common heart.

As the waitress brought out our entrees I watched the loving couple sample from each other's plates with giggles and smiles. I caught Tamika glancing over in my direction for my reaction. She certainly longed for that type of love and affection. I must admit that I desired it as well. Donavan had really won us over. He was a hard worker who had a great personality and heart to match. Dinner was truly a success and Beverly's face and attitude reflected that.

We got up to leave and Donavan suggested that he go pull the car around so that his "Yankee Queen" did not have to walk to the car. I joked that this guy was making me look bad in the chivalry department. He playfully punched my arm, smiled and ran out to his car. It came natural for him to do those things. I did not for one second think that he was putting on a show.

Beverly took this time to query us while Donavan was gone. "So, what do you guys think?" she asked, with a huge grin on her face.

Tamika answered first. "Does he have a brother?" she asked, giving Beverly a high-five.

"Unfortunately not in this state." Beverly then turned to me. "Czar, what do you think of Donavan?"

"What is there not to like about him, Beverly. I'm really happy for you. I see how he looks at you. Like there's not another woman in the whole world. Isn't that every woman's dream?"

"Oh, thank you for saying that Czar." Beverly's face was flustered as she went on. "You guys know that graduation is approaching and my mom will be here in a week. Well I'm going to break it off with Jonathan completely and start my new life with Donavan. No more escorting for me. I have a job interview set up the following week and it looks very promising."

We all exchanged hugs and congratulations to Beverly as we walked to the front of the restaurant. Donavan pulled up and came around to open Beverly's door. At that moment, a white Bentley Continental Coupe peeled out of the parking lot on squeaking tires. Beverly did not need to read the vanity plates that read WEILZ to know whose car that was. Tamika and I looked at each other and shook our heads in unison. Donavan was the only one not in the know. He looked at the car as it sped off into the distance.

"Man, I was just talking to that guy in the parking lot. He seemed really cool. I did not know he drove like an idiot. I guess when you spend a small fortune on a car like that, you can drive it any way you like." He went on, "It would take me a lifetime to afford one of those on what I make." He chuckled at his own joke.

There was grave concern on Beverly's face. How long had Jonathan been following her around? What did he talk to unassuming Donavan about in the parking lot?

Beverly entered the open passenger door that Donavan was holding. He shut the door behind her as she got in and then turned and shook my hand.-

He bid us farewell with a, "Nice to have met you Czar and you as well Tamika," his thick Jamaican accent engulfing his words. He hugged her goodbye then walked around to the driver's side. Beverly flashed me the universal "Call me" hand sign with her fingers cuffed and pinky plus thumb extended held up to her ear. I nodded with comprehension. They pulled away from the curb and out of the parking lot. Tamika and I walked to her car.

"That Jonathan is crazy Czar."

I did not say much other than, "Yeah, he's crazy okay."

I was thinking. I knew that Jonathan was going to be a problem since the evening at Tamika's condo when Beverly took his phone call. A man with money and power usually wanted things his way and did not let much stand in opposition to that.

# 11
# BLOOD ON STILETTOS

"Just when the caterpillar thought that his life was over;
he became a butterfly."

The signs were all around me. Earlier that morning I read a short but powerful quote on Facebook. It read, "What's not started today could not be finished tomorrow." I felt like it spoke directly to me. These social networks have created a multitude of quasi-philosophical gurus.

I had all the components of my luxury car service in place. All I had to do was step away from the escorting business. I did not want to leave any loose ends and Jonathan Weilz was more than a loose end. Beverly and I could not speak the night after dinner with Donavan since they spent the night together. I did not get an update from Beverly until noon the following day. She called me, franticly speaking on the phone.

"Beverly, slow down and tell me what's going on."

"Czar, Jonathan has been blowing up my phone since he burned rubber out of the parking lot at the restaurant the other night. I had to turn my phone off so that it would stop ringing. He filled my voicemail up with threatening messages. Listen."

Beverly pushed a sequence of numbers on her phone before the message began. "Look you little bitch, no one walks away from Jonathan Weilz like this. I had a nice talk with your truck driving boyfriend in the parking lot. Donavan right! After all I've done for you, you pick a broke truck driver over me! What is it, because I'm white? Is that it? Well I'm going to…." And just like that, the message was cut short since it was so long.

"Czar, listen to one of the other messages he left."

"Hey Beverly, I'm sorry for my previous message. I was angry, we need to talk. I'll do anything for you. What is it? More money? A car? What? I need to see you soon, I promise that…" And like the other messages, he was cut off in mid-sentence.

"Czar, all of his messages are like that. Either really angry and upset or apologetic and pitiful. He goes back and forth between the two emotions constantly. I can't risk Donavan finding out at all Czar! I'm sure he was in my apartment complex last night. I saw his black SUV two doors down with him just sitting in it."

"Okay Beverly, this is the plan. I'm going to grab Derrick and Malik then pay Jonathan a visit and let him know it's a wrap."

"Czar, I don't think I want it to come to that. Let that be the last resort."

"Look Beverly, I believe in being direct so that there is no misunderstanding from anyone."

"Let's just give it a couple of days and see what happens first Czar. My mom will be here in a week for the graduation. I don't need her walking into any drama."

"Okay, I'll follow your lead Beverly."

"Thank you Czar!"

"Beverly, I want you to know how proud I am of you. I've watched so many girls leave school and get trapped in this lifestyle. Now, here you are about to graduate at the top of your class. You're a testimony to other young women in this struggle.

I went and picked out a really nice Kenneth Cole suit for the occasion too Mama."

"I'm so excited Czar. You have no idea what this means to me and my family. I so wish that my father could be here to see it. All he ever spoke about was watching me walk across that stage on graduation day." I could clearly hear Beverly starting to tear up on the other line.

I chimed in, "Beverly I know he's looking down on you very proud right now."

In between a few sniffles, I could hear her agreeing with me. And as if something had jolted her memory she shouted "AND GUESS WHAT?!"

The excitement transferred to my reply, "WHAT?!"

"I'm going to be graduating Suma Cum Laude."

"Stop playing! A perfect 4.0? Yeah, your dad is certainly looking down from heaven a very proud father right now Beverly." I decided to end the conversation on a high note. "Look Beverly, I'm going to hit you up later. Call me if anything develops before that."

She said that she would then hung up the phone. I still felt uneasy about Jonathan but I was going to trust and respect Beverly's standpoint for now.

It was not long after hanging up the phone with Beverly that I got the good news that I'd been waiting for. Mr. Errol, the finance manager down at the Lincoln dealership, called and started the conversation with a big boisterous, "CONGRATULATIONS!"

I already knew what he was referring to. The dealership had agreed to finance a couple of vehicles for my luxury car service. I didn't say a word. I kind of just wanted to soak in the moment in silence. I could hear Mr. Errol on the other line, "Hello are you there? Mr. Mason are you there?"

I calmly said, "Yes, I'm here."

"Did you hear what I said? We are going to extend the credit request for the vehicles that you asked for."

"Thank you Mr. Errol."

"You don't sound too excited Mr. Mason."

"Believe me Mr. Errol, I'm extremely excited, believe me I am. It's all on the inside. I could burst right now Mr. Errol."

"What are you going to call your business Mr. Mason?"

"I'm going to call it Atlanta Luxury Livery."

"I like that. That's a great name. Well come down and sign the papers and take delivery of the vehicles the first chance that you get."

"Okay I will Mr. Errol, thanks again."

I hung the phone up and just exhaled. I had a new beginning in front of me. I felt a peace come over me. No more sidestepping what I do for a living. No more uncomfortable date questions where I dreaded the reaction to what I did to earn money. Maybe now I could have a regular relationship. I wanted out more than Tamika and Beverly put together. I'd been doing this way longer than both of them. I would have to make a clean break from the industry and the people altogether. I wanted the same thing for Beverly and Tamika.

Thinking of Tamika, I decided to give her a call. Her phone rang three times before she picked up.

"Hey Czar, guess who's ten thousand dollars richer?"

"NO!"

"YEAH! I just got off the phone with the DeKalb County Fugitive Task Force captain. He said that I'll be rewarded the money for the apprehension of Terrell. That bitch Princess inadvertently put money in my pocket; isn't that ironic! God has a great sense of humor. When I see that hoe I'm going to thank her." Tamika laughed at her own words. "Czar, you want to come to the mall with me to pick out a dress for Beverly's graduation?"

"What mall are you going to?"

Lenox Mall or Phipps Plaza since they are right across the street from each other we could hit both of them up."

"Aight, I'll come and scoop you up. Please be dressed and ready."

"You know I'll be ready Czar."

"Cool!" And with that I hung up the phone.

An hour later, Tamika and I were walking the corridors of Phipps Plaza. Tamika was beaming from ear to ear. I was certain that her reward check had something to do with it. She was less talkative than usual which was uncharacteristic for her. She seemed to have an outer glow with a smug look on her face.

I had to ask her, "Tamika, what's up?"

"What do you mean what's up?"

"I can tell that you're holding on to something." Tamika never broke stride as I spoke. "Listen, I know you well enough to know when something is afoot."

Tamika abruptly stopped and looked around as if she was about to tell me a governmental secret. In a hushed voice she said, "I'm done with the business Czar."

I didn't think I heard her correctly. I had to ask a second time. "What's that you said Tamika?"

This time in a regular overly loud voice she said, "I'm done with escorting!"

I believed her. I just had to know what the motivational factor was to do it now and so abruptly so I asked her. "Tamika, what prompted this change of heart?"

"Well it was not one particular thing, Czar. Beverly and I already knew we could not continue with this shit anyway. As human beings we always wait for the ideal moment to make change. I realized that the ideal moment to make change was in the here and now. Or we can always come up with a reason as to why to prolong change. There is never a more perfect moment for change than the present. I read this thing last night that said, 'What's not started today could not be finished tomorrow.' I felt like it spoke to me directly. I must admit that seeing the client and his family at the restaurant had a great impact on me as well."

I had to interrupt her for a minute. "Let me get this straight, Terrell's crazy ass almost killed you and that did not deter you from escorting? But you seeing the client and his family together really worked on your conscience enough to make you take the step to changing your mind?"

With a guilty smirk, Tamika answered. "Yeah, I mean I never saw that aspect of what we do. I believe in karma Czar, and the last thing I want is for my future husband to be seeing any escorts. I looked at his two beautiful children and I was ashamed for him and for myself; more so of myself. His wife was clueless! I would never want to be that woman."

"Wow, Tamika I understand!"

She turned and continued walking with me in tow. "Yeah Czar, I feel really good about my decision. I'm going back to school which was not even an option a few short months ago.

Now it's a reality. You and Beverly will be shopping for my graduation next!"

"Well I can't wait Tamika." We were walking side by side. I reached down and took her hand in mine. I gave her a squeeze of confidence. She flashed a smile of appreciation.

After walking in silence just peering through store windows, Tamika cleared her throat and spoke. "There's more Czar." She paused then continued, "I've learned from experience." She paused again, this time longer. The longer the pause, the more serious the nature of the subject.

"Tamika what is it?" The suspense was killing me. From her facial expression I could tell whatever it was, it was a touchy matter. I rubbed the small of her back and offered, "It's okay. It's okay."

I could see that Tamika was poising herself to say whatever she had to say. Then in one breathe she blurted out, "I'm going to join the church and get SAVED!"

I was perplexed by Tamika's reluctance to share that with me so I asked. "Why was that so hard to say, Tamika?"

"First off, I never really hear any of you guys talking about your spirituality. Secondly, I did not want to sound hypocritical because of the life I've led."

"Let me ask you something Tamika."

"Go ahead."

"Do you think the body of the church is made up of people who have been good Christians all of their lives?"

"No!"

"You're exactly right. Most people that have found God had to go through some things to begin searching for Him. One of the biggest sins is to judge someone else's relationship with

God. Only He knows what's in your heart. God will wash away all of your past transgressions."

Tamika smiled in agreement. "Czar, I had no idea that you went to church."

"Yeah I attend but I've been thinking about going more regularly."

"Well that's great because I was thinking of asking you and Beverly to come and get saved with me. I think at this juncture in all of our lives it would be really fitting to be reborn again together."

"With all of these mega churches in Georgia, how do you decide where to join?"

"What church do you go to?"

"I go to S.A.N.E. Church International (Saving A Nation Endangered) founded by Pastor Mason Betha."

"Who? The rapper Ma$e? Who used to be with Diddy? Shiny suits? Harlemworld Ma$e?"

"Yeah!"

"Where is his church at?"

"It was on Cheshire Bridge Road, now it's off of Piedmont. His vision is to bring young people like ourselves into the church who normally would not attend church."

"Okay, let's all make plans to go there then." Tamika seemed relieved as to my acceptance of her spiritual growth and even more that we had a house of worship in mind. There certainly was something different about Tamika today. Now it was so clear. She had grown out of the Tamika of yesterday and was ready to start a new chapter in her life. Now we had to get Beverly on board of this wind of change that was blowing.

The following day I got a much unexpected call from Donavan. I did not even know he had my number. His strong Jamaican accent clearly told me who it was right away.

"Czar, what a guan?" He put extra emphasis on the 'zar in my name.

"I'm good Donavan."

"I a fi get your number from Beverly. I hope you don't mind."

"Nah not at all, what's good?"

"Mi know how close you and Beverly is so mi thing you is the best man to talk to."

"Yeah, Donavan go on."

"Mi have two things I want to chat to you about concerning Beverly."

Immediately my stomach got tight at the thought of Donavan asking me the unthinkable about Beverly. I stuttered in response, "Wha… what's your concerns Donavan?"

"Well, the first one is, I don't have a lot of money for a graduation gift. Mi would love to take her to my homeland of Jamaica as a graduation gift, but mi can't afford that. So what's the next ting you think she would like?"

My tension was at ease now, what a relief! I was not going to be the one to share Beverly's secret with Donavan. "Donavan that's easy. Beverly just wants your love. So whatever you do, give it a real personal touch."

"Come on Czar, mi need more help than that, brother."

"Okay Donavan, I know for a fact that she's been wanting to visit Savannah for a while now. So I suggest a road trip weekend getaway just the two of you guys."

"Oh mi like that Czar! Mi like that. Very romantic that."

I could picture Donavan's broad smile on the other end of the phone. He was content with my suggestion. Soon after that I could hear and feel the shift in his energy. The second part of his concerns seemed to carry grave sadness. I braced myself and began to search my mind's eyes for the right words.

"Czar, mi not sure but mi feel like Beverly is hiding something from I and I. She talk on the phone in di bathroom with de door lock for long times. Mi catch her keep looking out di window every two minutes. Mi don't know if she seeing another man or not."

"Well Donavan let me start by letting you know that I know Beverly well enough to know that she's in love with you."

My words offered no concession to Donavan. He let out one long, "Steups"[1] and said, "So what is going on, man?"

I felt his pain but it was not my place to speak on it either way. "Look Donavan, I'm going to have a talk with Beverly for you. How's that?"

There was a silence on the other line then a reluctant, "Okay, Czar. Let me know if you find out anything, brother!"

Damn, why did he have to put that "brother" in there? I felt guilty for knowing the truth of the matter. "I will Donavan." He hung up.

---

[1] Steups - /ste-oops/ sound or expression used in the Caribbean and South America wherein one would suck his or her teeth to show disapproval or unacceptance.

Beverly, unbeknownst to me, had come up with her own resolve for dealing with Jonathan. She really was under the impression that she could reason with Jonathan. She had seen him in his most vulnerable positions, no pun intended, and thought that that same control transferred into the real world. The fantasy began and ended in his makeshift dungeon in his house. He was still that controlling, out-of-control teenager that violated Carmen so violently years ago. Beverly had a non-confrontational personality and wanted to please both her need to quietly end this chapter in her life and not piss off Jonathan after all he had done for her. I read a long time ago that you could not serve two masters; it was all or nothing! Jonathan had been blackmailing Beverly with threats of going to Donavan exposing her as an escort. That was Beverly's worst fear.

Beverly had been secretly rendezvousing with Jonathan for the past week. That would explain Donavan's newfound suspicions that prompted the phone call to me. It would also explain why she did not want me confront Jonathan. Beverly really thought that she could reason with this egotistical psycho. She was making a big mistake. Appeasing Jonathan was a short term fix. He would continue to hold the threats of telling Donavan over her head, and she knew this.

Beverly had gotten dressed and prepared to have an early dinner with Jonathan. Jonathan had the car service pick her up at her place. She had no idea where she would be dining tonight. There was a lump in her throat as she thought about how much she wanted to put an end to this cat and mouse game with

Jonathan. The driver came around to her door and greeted her "Good evening ma'am."

Beverly nodded and mustered up a kind smile despite the contrary feeling boiling over inside of her stomach. Beverly sat in complete silence as the Lincoln Towne Car traveled north on Piedmont Road. The driver glanced up at his rearview mirror, surveying Beverly occasionally. Beverly just stared at the passing Atlanta landmarks emptily, her eyes never really focusing on anything. It was all just a blur. She was composing the dialogue that would appeal to Jonathan's sense of compassion. With Jonathan's wealth, he could have just about any woman he wanted. He opted to have things that resisted him. The driver made a left onto Pharr Road by a BP gas station.

Beverly's curiosity was satisfied when they pulled into Prici's parking lot. "We're here ma'am!"

Beverly politely smiled back to the driver and said, "Thank you," while rustling through her pocketbook. She plucked out a ten dollar tip for the driver. She folded the bill and cuffed it in her hand mob style.

When the driver came around to open her door she stepped out and attempted to thrust the money into his hand. "No ma'am, Mr. Weilz has taken care of everything already."

"I want you to have it."

"But he…"

Beverly cut him off and said, "I'll feel more comfortable if you did."

Reluctantly, he outstretched his hand and said, "Thank you, ma'am."

Beverly's eyes scanned the parking lot and saw Jonathan's Bentley Coupe. He was there already. She walked into the dimly lit restaurant and was immediately greeted by the hostess. "This way, Mr. Weilz has been expecting you."

The restaurant was to capacity even that early in the evening. They approached the table and Beverly could see that Jonathan had finished a bottle of wine by himself. Jonathan stood up and greeted Beverly with a soft kiss on her cheek. Dinner was more Beverly's idea than Jonathan's. She figured a nice public place would be as easy a place to sever ties with Jonathan, diplomatically. From the moment that Beverly sat down, she realized that Jonathan was a bit more hyperactive than usual. His nose was running and he had a case of the sniffles. There was no doubt in her mind that he was on cocaine and high as hell right now. She asked herself why she didn't ask the driver to return for her. Beverly began regretting making dinner plans already.

Jonathan spoke first. "How are you my dear?" His words were laced with insincerity.

"I could be much better, Jonathan."

"What do you mean much better? Isn't your garbage-man boyfriend making you happy?"

The thought of Jonathan even referring to Donavan made her blood crawl. Beverly understood this was neither the time nor the place to show emotions. She did not want to provoke Jonathan either. Beverly decided to stay on task. Beverly knew how much of an ego Jonathan had so she wanted to play on that. "Jonathan you are a wonderful guy and any woman would be happy to have you."

You could see Jonathan's posture change and he was much more comfortable with Beverly's praise. She continued stroking his id. "If we would have met under different circumstances I would have loved to be with you."

"It does not matter to me how we met, Beverly."

The waitress walked over just then. "Would you guys like to order?"

Jonathan did not wait for Beverly to order. He announced that he would have his regular. The waitress obviously knew what that was because she scribbled something on her order form.

Beverly's index finger stopped midway down the menu page, "I'll have this," she said, pointing at the blackened salmon with potatoes and vegetables.

"And bring another bottle of wine too," Jonathan added.

The waitress looked at Beverly. "Will you be having wine as well?"

Before she could answer, Jonathan insisted that the waitress bring her a glass as well.

The couple to their right was visibly annoyed by Jonathan's loud tone of voice. The waitress walked away to retrieve their orders.

Beverly took a deep breath and looked Jonathan square in his blood-shot eyes. "Look Jonathan, I'm here to find a happy medium that would work for both of us."

"What do you mean?"

"I want to compromise with you!"

"Beverly, you're not in a position to compromise. I want you to think about who's been paying your rent? Who made it possible for you to get that fancy degree you earned? Now you want to cast me aside. Well it doesn't work like that!"

"Jonathan, I could find you another girl."

"What you think, I can't find my own? Let's be clear Beverly, you're going to do as I tell you to do. That's the trade off with this sugar-daddy arrangement."

Beverly's eyes fell to the floor. She could hear the finality in his voice. All she was trying to do was buy herself some time. She knew after graduation she would be moving in with Donavan. She would just have to maintain the peace for a couple of weeks.

The waitress brought out the second bottle of wine and a glass for Beverly. She poured them both a glass and walked away. Jonathan held up his glass to toast. Beverly decided to humor him and did the same. "To my future graduate and lover."

Beverly averted eye contact while Jonathan touched their wine glasses, with the glasses clinking in vain. She had her phone on silent but looking down at it in her pocketbook, she could see that she had seven missed calls. Four of them were from Donavan, two from Tamika and one next to Czar's name. She wondered how this must look to Donavan, unanswered phone calls and unbeknown whereabouts! Beverly stumbled through dinner with a lot of small talk and false smiles, convincing Jonathan that she could make it the way it used to be between them in the past if only he would be patient. Again, Beverly was just trying to buy the few weeks that she needed to make a clean break from Jonathan. Beverly decided to play the ultimate courtier to Jonathan despite it being an act. The mask she wore on her face did not reflect all that was going on inside of her. Her heart and thoughts were with Donavan. She just wanted to bawl out loud. Sitting across the table from Jonathan was nauseating to her. Still she sat, smiled and nodded in agreement with him.

Beverly's intention was to have dinner then head back to her place and spend time with Donavan. It was now obvious to her that Jonathan wanted her to come home with him, no doubt for one of his freak sessions. She was resolved to get it over with. Beverly raised her index finger in the air to get the passing waitress's attention.

"May we have the check please?"

"No desert for you?"

"No thank you, we plan on having desert at home if you know what I mean," Beverly responded, glaring her eyes at Jonathan flirtatiously and sealing it with a wink.

"Girl, I know exactly what you mean. I'll be back with the check in a sec."

Jonathan perked up and sat straight in his chair. Beverly's innuendo stroked his ego and turned him on. What Jonathan did not know was Beverly had something a little different in mind than he did. Beverly had never gotten into her role as sadomasochist with Jonathan but tonight she certainly would. She intended to inflict as much pain as possible on him—fuck the safe word.

Jonathan paid the bill and stumbled to the entrance where the valets were. While the young valet dashed off with the ticket in hand, Beverly stood arm-in-arm, steadying Jonathan. He visibly had too much to drink and God knows what else. You wouldn't be able to tell Beverly's intention from her demeanor and attentiveness to Jonathan's every need. Feeling the vibrating silent phone in her purse just infuriated her more and more; undoubtedly it was Donavan. Beverly was risking losing the love of her life for this fucker! She was boiling on the inside while maintaining an angelic smile on the outside. She drove them to his place in his car since he had had one too many drinks.

Pulling up to his home, she parked and hurried to the passenger's door to help him out. The tapping of her high heels against the cobblestone driveway was very distinct in the late night air. Jonathan slumped over on Beverly's shoulder attempting to kiss her as she opened the car door. Pulling away, she said, "Hold on, we'll have plenty of time for that."

A smile curled on Jonathan's lips. "That's what I'm talking about baby."

The thought of anyone other than Donavan calling her baby made Beverly's blood crawl. *I got your baby asshole,* ran through Beverly's thoughts. Still very much in character, Beverly draped Jonathan's right arm over her shoulder then steadied him with her own arm around his waist. They walked step-in-step with each other, into the house through the front door. Beverly directed him straight up the stairs to the dungeon room. Donavan's excitement could be felt growing in his pants as he pressed up against Beverly's body. With cocaine and alcohol already in his system he was ready to satisfy his sexual vice now.

Jonathan took off his shirt and made himself comfortable while waiting for Beverly to join him in the playroom. He was sitting in the dimly lit room in total silence, the quiet deafening to his ears. The room was completely still except when he attempted to stand up. The five minutes Beverly had been gone seemed much, much longer to Jonathan in his drug and alcohol stupor. He was growing impatient. Jonathan began hollering at the top of his lungs for Beverly. "BEVERLY! BEVERLY!"

Just as he opened his mouth to yell Beverly's name again, she appeared in the doorway of the playroom. Jonathan was taken aback by what he saw. Beverly's silhouette and shapely body was outlined by the light in the background of the hallway. Even though Jonathan had seen her in full costume many times in the past, there was certainly something different about her tonight. She stood six feet in her five-inch patent leather knee-high boots. Black fishnet stockings protruded from the shiny boots up into matching patent leather hot pants. Beverly's washboard stomach was exposed, the ripples of defined abs very visible. She had on matching black elbow-length gloves as well. Her makeup was darker around her eyes. She had transformed herself into total dominatrix mode. To complete her ensemble, she revealed the eight-inch leather flogger with tassels at its end, which she had concealed behind her back.

Jonathan's eyes widened, his frustration giving way to excitement and anticipation. Beverly began to approach him with slow deliberate steps, never uttering a word. Her eyes were locked in on Jonathan's.

"Yes baby, give it to daddy."

"I'll give it to you alright!" In one fluid motion, Beverly ripped the three hundred dollar custom-tailored button-up shirt off of Jonathan's back. The buttons popped off in sequence, one after the other, scattering into different corners of the room. Jonathan was totally submissive to each and every demand of Mistress Beverly.

"Turn around and put your hands into the straps."

Jonathan complied. With his hands extended over his head and bound with the Velcro straps, his entire back was now exposed to Beverly's whip. Beverly took a step back and wound her arm up like a major league pitcher. The leather whip crashed violently against his back. Even in the dimly lit room, the red welt across his back was very visible. Jonathan's eyes rolled to the back of his head in ecstasy. "Thank you ma'am may I have another."

His words infuriated Beverly. This fucker was not supposed to be enjoying this. Beverly once again drew back her arm and began wailing onto Jonathan's bare back. It was if she had blacked out—her body was present but her mind was certainly elsewhere. Beverly had bottled up all the emotions of her actions as an escort and unfortunately for Jonathan, it was all pouring out now. She had so many questions of herself. How did she give Jonathan so much power over her life? Why did she give Jonathan so much control over her? She acted like she liked him while she resented him, the money and more importantly, she resented herself. MONEY! Because of money! The thought of giving her body for money sickened her stomach for the very first time since she had learned to separate herself from that person taking calls. She continued blindly lashing at Jonathan's now raw, bleeding back.

Jonathan's cries to stop went unheard by Beverly. It was as if she was in a trance and was not even present. Jonathan was yelling, "Carmen! Carmen!" from the top of his lungs. The safe word turned out not to be so safe.

Beverly was sweating profusely. You could not distinguish the tears on her face from beads of sweat. The beating seemed to have sobered Jonathan right up. Jonathan struggled with the Velcro clasped around his wrist until he freed himself. Beverly had not noticed his hands were free until it was way too late. Jonathan open-handed slapped her with a blow to the left side of her face. It was only then that Beverly came back to reality.

"Mothafucker!! My daddy never hit me!" She lunged at Jonathan with pure rage. His six-foot-three frame towered over Beverly. He quickly grabbed her and applied a sleepy hold around her neck. Jonathan tightened his arms and began rocking back and forth to induce Beverly into sleep. Beverly felt the air leaving her body and began getting light-headed. If she passed out, she would be totally helpless.

She mustered up all the strength left in her as she raised her right foot and began jabbing the dagger-like heel of her stilettos into Jonathan's shin. Beverly's heel pierced into the fleshy tissue of Jonathan's lower leg. Releasing Beverly from his grips and crying out in utter pain while reaching for his bleeding leg, Jonathan fell backwards onto the floor. Even though she was now free from Jonathan's hold, Beverly stood buckled over in the same spot, gasping for a full breath. Five seconds longer in that hold and Beverly certainly would have been rendered unconscious. Hunched over, attempting to compose herself, Beverly noticed Jonathan's blood all over her stilettos. There was a blood droplet trail from Beverly's shoes to the spot where Jonathan was now agonizing in pain, holding his leg in an attempt to stop the bleeding. Beverly looked up at her own image in the mirror on the wall. Even in the dimly lit room, the lacerations around her neck were prominent. *How the fuck am I going to explain this to Donavan?*

Now that she caught her breathe, the anger and rage returned. She took a few steps in Jonathan's direction and just when he turned her way, she kicked him in his face. The instep of her foot struck him directly on the bridge of his nose surely breaking it.

"I'm going to KILL you you fucking whore!" he screamed while all the while clutching his face. "I OWN YOU BITCH!!"

The gash in his leg did not seem so bad now that blood was spouting out of his nose. Beverly positioned herself and wound her foot up for a second assault. This time though, Jonathan would be ready. He caught her foot in midair leaving her to balance herself on the other leg. She was successful at balancing for all of five awkward seconds then she fell hard on her back. She was now on his level! Jonathan dragged her across the floor to him. He then crawled on top of her and got right in her face. Beverly could smell the alcohol from dinner mixed with blood on his breath but could not make out a word that he was saying, being so close to him as he yelled so loud it was inaudible. She could not kick or fight with his weight on top of her.

"You broke my nose bitch," was followed with a borage of punches to Beverly's face. His first shot landed directly onto her left eye. It instantaneously blackened and swelled shut. His second blow landed square on her jaw, knocking several of her teeth out. Even though Beverly lay helpless beneath his weight, he never relented. Jonathan continued to beat her motionless body. The pretty private school girl from Chicago was unrecognizable.

Jonathan finally stumbled to his feet, still nursing both his leg and his broken nose. He got up and sat on his contraption that had brought him so much pleasure in the past. The room of pleasure ironically became the room of pain tonight. Jonathan's gaze landed on the sprawled out body in his house as he came to and thought, *What have I done?*

Jonathan staggered to his feet and exited the room, frantically searching for his cell phone. He needed to talk to Joseph, the pilot of the company's jet, to let him know to get over to DeKalb Airport and prep the plane for an emergency takeoff. As far as Jonathan knew, Beverly was dead. But was she?

Beverly had blacked out from the blunt force trauma to her head, blood matting her long hair. She regained consciousness minutes later, lying flat on her back, looking up at what seemed to be a spinning ceiling. She only had sight in her right eye which was blurred by the blood in it. The whole scene seemed surreal and somewhat like an out-of-body experience for Beverly. While her mind seemed to be fully aware, her body and spirit were frozen. She could hear Jonathan's voice off in the distance in another room but was paralyzed with fear to even turn her neck in that direction. At that moment Jonathan stopped his conversation and his movement. She knew he had paused to look in on her from the room down the hall. After a still thirty seconds, which felt more like thirty minutes, he resumed with the person on the phone. She could only make out bits and pieces of his conversation.

"No, it would be me alone... I'll let you know when I get there." It made no sense to her. Beverly's mind began to race. Should I lay here and play dead until he's gone? What if he comes back in here and checks my vitals? He'll surely kill me then.

Beverly knew she was in the first room at the top of the stairs. If she could just make it down the stairs, the front door would offer her freedom. If she was going to make a run for the door she would have to be swift. Beverly regretfully looked at the boots on her feet. Those heels were not going to help any more than they already had. She would have to zip then down and ease them off, for her dash. Jonathan was still on the phone but his voice was much more muffled. He must have been in the master bathroom within his room. Now was her chance! She reached with her right hand to zip down her left boot then mirrored the action to get her right boot off. She used the toe-to-heel tactic to kick them off. It was now or never. Beverly raised her upper torso, blood that had accumulated in her mouth and face spilling to the floor in a puddle. She had no idea of the extent of injuries which she had suffered. Sitting up made her dizzy. She spat out a loose tooth to the floor. She was in pain. The sight of all the blood made it hurt that much more.

Beverly was now on her feet and Jonathan was nowhere in sight. Darting to what she thought was the open door at full speed, she hit the wall. Beverly's partial sight in one eye was giving her double vision. Unfortunately, she picked the wrong door. The noise of crashing into the wall brought Jonathan running into the hall. Beverly's subsequent go at the door was met with a more favorable result this time. But it was a little too late. Jonathan caught her at the top of the stairs.

"I thought you were dead, whore." He was holding her, arms pinned to her side, facing him.

Beverly did not answer, at least not with words. She spat blood into his face.

Jonathan's eyes were totally empty when he thrust Beverly down the steep flight of stairs. Beverly never had a chance. She fell backwards directly on her vertebrae. Beverly's neck was broken before her body settled at the base of the steps. Jonathan casually walked down the stairs and checked her pulse at her neck and wrist. Yes, Beverly was certainly dead.

# 12
# REFORMED

*"You can't keep doing the same thing
expecting a different result."*

Beverly's body lay on the cold marble floor of Jonathan's house until the next day when a delivery man with a package, peered through the door's glass pane and saw her. The detective had called me from her cell phone log of missed calls. He asked me to come down and positively identify Beverly's body. Every fiber in my body wanted it to be someone else, but in my heart of hearts I knew it was her. She had not returned more than a half dozen calls of mine, which was uncharacteristic of her. Driving to Fulton County Examiner's Office was the longest ten minute drive I'd ever experienced. I simply did not want to get there.

Viewing Beverly's dead body was probably one of the most difficult things I've ever had to do. It was like losing a sister that I never had. I called Tamika as I walked out of the coroner's building. Her phone barely rang before she was on the line.

"Hello," she answered in a somber voice.

"Hey, Tamika."

She never greeted me. "Have you heard from Beverly?" Without waiting for a reply, she went on. "I've been calling her phone all night. She's not with Donavan. He's been calling me looking for her."

The picture of Beverly's naked corpse lying on that sheet of metal was still fresh in my mind from minutes ago. I was in a haze. This was not happening. But it was! Tamika's chatting had not stopped but I did not hear much of it. I had zoned out. I could not bring myself to tell her of Beverly's murder over the phone. I just couldn't. "Tamika, where are you?"

"I'm at my place."

"Okay, I'm on my way there right now."

I can't say that I even remember driving to Tamika's place. I do remember hesitantly knocking on her front door. The door swung open. Tamika stood there in a t-shirt and panties. I did not have to say a word. I guess my demeanor, facial expression and spirit said it all. Tamika initially gave me a quizzical gaze, jerking her neck back and squinting her eyes, then her brow wrinkled followed by a contorted expression. She knew from reading my body language, that her sister and best friend was dead. Her open palms came up over her face. She involuntarily fell to her knees and the most sorrowful wail that a human being could excrete came out of her body.

I'd been holding back my own tears from the time I had spoken to the detective early in the day. Whether or not I wanted to cry did not matter; the streams of tears were coming down my cheeks now. I knelt down in front of Tamika and hugged her while we both were on our knees. We rocked back and forth in an attempt to comfort each other.

I spent the rest of the day with Tamika at her place. We were each other's support system. We ordered food but neither of us had an appetite. The day was a huge roller coaster of emotions. We spent time laughing at the good times we'd shared with

Beverly then the realization would set in that we wouldn't have any more of those times with her. The toughest part of the day was making that dreaded phone call to Beverly's mom in Chicago. I did not want her to hear it from the police. I normally didn't drink but this situation warranted that I had a double shot. I poured the coconut Ciroc in the glass straight, no ice or chaser. I motioned to offer Tamika one as well. She shook her head no. I held my glass up to honor Beverly and threw it back. I was ready now. Tamika and I held hands as I dialed the number and placed the call on speaker. Tamika had spoken to her in the past more than I had, so I let her take the lead.

"Hello Mrs. Copeland."

"Hello Tamika, haven't heard your voice in a while."

Tamika bit her bottom lip and looked at me, before replying. "I have Czar on the line as well Mrs. Copeland."

"How are you doing ma'am?"

"Good Czar, good."

The awkward pause in between our words caused Mrs. Copeland to ask, "Is everything okay with Beverly?" There is no way to ever tell a parent that their child is dead. She echoed her concerns again. "Is everything okay with Beverly?"

Tamika looked at me I looked back at Tamika. I took in a deep breath and the words just came out of my mouth. "Mrs. Copeland, there's no easy way to tell you this but Beverly is no longer with us."

I would have felt much better if I would have heard her fall out balling, but she didn't. The shock of it was too much for her. It was caught in her chest and she could not get it out. "You must be mistaken, Czar." Denial is always our first line of coping with tragedy. "Are you sure? It can't be her. I'm going to hang up and call her phone right now!"

"Mrs. Copeland. Mrs. Copland!" She was not hearing me over her own voice. I had to raise my voice. "MRS. COPELAND!" Getting her attention now, I spoke in the calmest voice I could find within me. "I identified her body earlier today ma'am."

And that's when I heard the balling into the phone. The initial shock was gone; she could let it out. I heard her phone fall to the ground and could hear her grief on the other line. After a few minutes of listening I realized she was not coming back. I hung up the line.

Tamika's hands were palm-to-palm, held up to her face as if she was praying, with a never-ending stream of tears cascading down her face. I stared in her direction and gestured to the phone with my eyes. She knew exactly what I was saying without uttering a word. She would have to make the call to Donavan and tell him.

My heart was now in my throat after hearing a mother's pain of losing a child. I hate being the bearer of bad news! Tamika closed her eyes, started saying some words under her breath and then proceeded to dial Donavan's number.

"'Ello." I could hear his thick Jamaican accent from where I was standing. "Where Beverly daia?"

"Donavan I need you to sit down."

"Mi nah want to sit down. Where Beverly daia?"

"Donavan, Beverly is dead."

"A how ya mean Beverly a fi dead? A who do this? Mi a fi kill dem dead, ya hear. BUMBA CLOUT."

The more upset Donavan got, it became more difficult to understand him. "Ras Clout! Mi Queen a fi gone. No, no, no." His anger ran deep from his soul. I could never imagine the pain that's involved with losing a lover. He came back to the phone and spoke into it gently, almost a whisper now. "Mi gaan, mi gaan."

Tamika instinctively knew that he was saying bye, and she hung up the phone. Her eyes were welled up again. She ran over to me and threw her arms around my shoulders and buried her head into my chest. I settled my chin at the top of her head and lovingly squeezed her. She squeezed back. We stood there in an embrace for a while until she looked up and kissed me deep and long. I was taken off guard and shocked at first, then found myself kissing her back.

Damn, I remembered the first day I saw her; it seemed so long ago. I thought she was so pretty. I sat in my truck and played it cool. I thought about her sexually on much too many occasions to admit. Now she was in my arms. I'd declined her advances so many other times. It felt different now. She took me by the hand and led me over to the sofa which faced the open patio. The drapes were drawn open as well. It felt like the whole city could look in at us. We sat down facing each other about a foot apart. Tamika pulled her t-shirt off over her head exposing the most two perfect breasts that you would ever want to see. Her nipples were already erect. She leaned in and kissed me really soft. I felt my heart pace increase. She must have noticed it too because she smiled at me and kissed me deeper and more passionately than before. Her right hand ran beneath my shirt finding my right nipple. She pushed her weight on top of me causing me to fall back on the sofa. She was now on top of me. We were in a passionate deep kiss when her tongue began going south. She bit and teased my neck with mini bites that were followed with soft kisses. Tamika was very sensual. I could feel her grinding her midsection on my knee. She continued south where her tongue found my right nipple. That was my spot and she seemed to know it, glancing up at me with an "I know" look which really turned me on. The growing bulge in my jeans began to get uncomfortable. I motioned her to get up. She knew what I wanted to do. Reaching for my shoes that were still on, she opted to pull them off by the heels instead of unlacing them. I wriggled my pants past my waist and she did the rest. Grabbing my erect penis in her hand through my boxers, Tamika looked at me and said, "I like."

I blushed at the compliment. Beverly's death was looming in the air. The reality of her being gone, even looking at her cold body on that sheet of metal had not fully registered with me yet. Tamika picked up that my mind was elsewhere. I did not want any grief sex! Was I taking advantage of her in such a delicate place? Was she taking advantage of me?

Still holding my dick, Tamika spoke. "You okay? Do you want to do this?"

"That's what I was about to ask you."

"Czar I've been wanting to do this from the moment I met you. Don't act like you don't know this." She started to say something else but I placed my index finger on her lips. She got the message. She would be quiet.

Tamika took my finger into her mouth and began seductively and gently sucking on it all the while maintaining deep eye contact with me. That went on for a minute or so. She then took my hand and guided it down into her moist panties. My index and middle finger were now massaging her clit in a soft circular motion. Tamika began panting and breathing heavily. She was rubbing her nipples and gyrating with the rhythm of my fingers up against her wet kitty. It was more than obvious that Tamika was ready. She jumped up from the sofa saying, "I'll be right back," and ran into her bedroom.

I watched her cross the room as her perfect C-cups bounced with every step. Just as fast as she had exited she was back, arm extended in my direction. In her hand was a gold foil wrapper.

"Yes a condom, thank you."

"I figured you were an extra-large," she commented, glancing down at my erect penis.

"Good choice."

What Tamika and I shared for the next few hours was simply blissful. The thing about it was this: If we would have acted on our attraction to each other much earlier, it would not have been the same. We had time to get to know and care for each other. As we both lay on the sofa enjoying the afterglow of our passion, the news came on. Beverly's death led the headlines. The anchor lady did say that Jonathan Weilz was the primary suspect. The plane's tail number had been tracked to a small private airport outside of Mexico City. When the media interviewed the pilot he did confirm that he had dropped Mr. Weilz off in Mexico. I shook my head, thinking out loud. "He could be anywhere in the world at this point."

Tamika concurred with me. "Bastard!"

There was now a worldwide manhunt for Jonathan Weilz. Donavan, Tamika and I were standing at Beverly's grave site in Allerton Ridge Cemetery five days later.

Allerton Ridge Cemetery was in Boilingbrook about seven miles from the home that Beverly had grown up in and where her father now laid in rest. Her mother had spent many a Sundays visiting his grave site. Now his little girl would be laid to rest next to him.

It was a bright sunny day and the temperature in Illinois was ideal, neither too hot nor too cool. It was a very small intimate gathering. The pastor was a dark-skinned man about five-foot-eight and thirty pounds overweight with a gravelly voice. If I had to guess his age I would have placed him around late fifties to early sixties. As he spoke about Beverly and made broad typical comments about her, I realized he could be talking about any young lady her age. I couldn't help but to stop and wonder if he had ever even met Beverly. I stood there looking at her open coffin, fighting back tears thinking to myself about how fragile and mortal we really are.

I had permanently propped Tamika up on my left side as she wailed and cried for our lost sister. Donavan was on my right, crying just as much as Tamika. I felt cheated, standing there being strong for everyone else. I wanted my moment of pure vulnerability to grieve for Beverly, whom I loved much more than I had really known. I stopped and looked around. I could not hear anything as I watched the pastor's mouth formulating words. It was like I was an outside observer taking in the whole scene. I had never thought of the girls at the agency in terms of having family and loved ones. As my eyes scanned over the faces and bodies dressed in black, it dawned on me. These people did not know who Beverly was. Yes, in terms of relationship and titles—cousins, aunts, uncles, etc. But they did not know the beauty of her spirit and drive.

The bond that links your true family is not one of blood but of respect and joy in each other's life. As that thought collided with the silence playing in my head, I looked up and saw one solitary white dove flying above our heads in a circular pattern.

The next word that became audible to me was the pastor's voice saying "AMEN!" As if on cue, the white dove soared high and to the East. My eyes were transfixed on the bird as it flew away and eventually turned into a small dot in my eye's view, slowly disappearing.

Beverly was free. Beverly's mother returned to Atlanta with us. Her funeral was only days prior of her graduation. We sat out on the lush green lawn of Spelman's campus behind the graduating class. The sun was out but again, not hot at all. There was a tremendous energy in the air. There must have been at least a thousand people in attendance. Caps and gowns with smiling faces plastered the stage. The empty seat to my right was once occupied by Mrs. Copeland who was now waiting backstage to hear her daughter's name called so that she could receive her degree. Tamika and Donavan were to the left of me with proud looks permanently engraved on their faces. The commentator was calling names in alphabetical order so we were in anticipation. Evidently everyone else was too. Then the moment came when, "Beverly Copeland," blared through the PA system. Mrs. Copeland emerged from behind the curtain on the stage and with her head held high, proudly marched across that stage to receive her beloved daughter's degree. There was an enormous roar from the graduating class. They were on their feet giving a standing ovation. Beverly was truly loved by her classmates and peers. Mrs. Copeland shook the Dean's hand and received the degree. The crowd got even louder. As she approached the podium she adjusted the height of the mic. She looked out at the rows of students, families, staff and well-wishers and simply said, "Thank you for giving my daughter an education."

There were no tears in her words, just pride. The crowd erupted again as she exited off stage. There were tears in the eyes of some of the students and faculty members. Mrs. Copeland returned to her seat where we all took turns holding and looking at the beautifully framed diploma.

"She did it."

"Yes, she did Mrs. Copeland."

It was as if Tamika and I had an unspoken understanding after graduation day. Neither one of us mentioned the agency or anyone affiliated with it. We both just ignored the office calls until they became fewer then faded into nonexistence. You can't keep doing the same thing expecting a different result. That is the clinical definition of insanity.

# 13

# ATLANTA

"Life sometimes imitates art."

I t had been six months since Beverly's murder and not a day went past without her smile crossing my mind. She was a beautiful human being. I didn't speak to her mother as much as I had in the first few months after her funeral. I made a mental note to phone her later that day. Jonathan Weilz had been arrested in Thailand and was being questioned in the disappearance of a young Thailander sex worker and the murder of another girl. He was vigorously fighting extradition back to the States to face Beverly's murder charges. We all just wanted a sense of closure. The only way that closure would be possible would be to see Jonathan Weilz on death row.

The prosecuting attorney said that he'd seemed extraditions tied up in courts for years on end. The fact that Jonathan had the means for the best defense team did not help either. His arrest in Thailand made national news. It was something about money and murder that captured the media's attention. Looking at the news report and seeing him in handcuffs felt good. He had grown a lot of facial hair and lost a considerable amount of weight, no doubt in an attempt to disguise himself from law enforcement. It did not work.

I clicked off the television and looked around the office. Atlanta Luxury Livery was running strong and building a regular clientele now. I was really fortunate to hire some quality drivers that shared my vision for the company. The best news of all was that Tamika was accepted and enrolled at Spelman and worked in the office with me on a part-time basis. When I listened to her answer calls, set appointments, and schedule drivers, I couldn't believe it was the same girl from the West End. To say that I was proud of her would be a gross understatement. We'd been dating ever since that afternoon of passion on her couch. We even talked about us moving in together. There was no denying our connection from day one. I had to overcome my own reservation of being in a relationship with a, "Whore."

Tamika was no whore. Like so many economically challenged people, she was looking for an easy way out when in reality it was actually the harder way in. I came to terms with the whole notion that I was not trying to turn a hoe into a housewife. I saw her for who she was. What she had done did not define her. Where would any of us be if we were defined by our past? It was very clear now that what we shared back then was more than grief sex.

I sat there reflecting and it was like Tamika was reading my mind. She walked over and said, "You like how I'm handling business, huh?"

She playfully massaged my shoulders as she passed through to go to the other room.

I called after her, answering her back. "Yeah, I love how you're handling things, Mama."

I fell back into thought. We lived in such a misogynistic society that told young women to, "Use what you got to get what you want," or another popular adage, "If you got it flaunt it."

Many of our young women's worth is boxed into how pretty their faces or how shapely their bodies are. The media controls the narrative and that narrative is being taken as gospel by the youths. No longer do the young people have an original thought. Their opinions are given to them whether on a conscious level or a subconscious level. Consumerism and materialism is the absolute, while character and integrity takes a back seat.

I have a lot of single female friends that are really frustrated with the dating scene and the pool of options that are available to them. We get into these very spirited debates on the state of relationships. My stance is that most women are more interested in what a man drives instead of finding out what drives the man. Atlanta is one of those places where what you do dictates how you're treated. People here worship empty titles. I advise my single female friends to look for character and drive in a man. With those components intact, all the other smaller things will fall into place. When someone really holds themself in high esteem then and only then, will he or she not settle for anything less.

Until these young women take their self-worth out of their hips and bust line, they'll continue to search out employment at escort agencies. I occasionally go online and browse the escort sites, craigslist and back pages. Coming across title headings like, "Young and Ready," and, "New to the Business," I can't help but wonder if they really know what they're getting into. It's like opening up Pandora's Box which is not that easy to close. I am astonished at the rates some of these girls are offering their services for in these ads—young girls rendering sexual acts as low as thirty and forty dollars. If that's not an indication outside of a moral one that it's not worth it, I don't know what is.

Atlanta has more strip clubs per capita than any other city in the United States. The city of Atlanta issues thousands of dance and escort permits per year. I have found, not in all cases but in a disproportionate number of cases, that erotic dancing is the gateway to other illicit activities within the sex industry. Most of the girls that came to the escort service were dancers at strip clubs. The same held true for the ones that ventured into the porn industry. The FBI has named Atlanta the number one sex destination within the United States borders. Much of the nation's sex trafficking laws were written based on cases that had originated here in Atlanta.

Atlanta is one of the places where the pimp culture is still romanticized. Names like, "Sir Charles," are floated on the streets and in pop music. Sir Charles was known for having each one of his girls brand herself with a tattoo proclaiming, *Sir Charles* in a fancy script on her body. Then there is "Batman," who was known for his notorious, brutal abuse of his prostitutes. Mike Spades is now serving a fifteen year sentence for sex trafficking and exploitation of a minor.

Atlanta has a diverse and growing ethnic makeup. With the influx of diversity comes the element of global human trafficking as well. There's a large Latino community northeast of the city—Norcross, Doraville, Buford Highway and Lawrenceville—where enclaves of illegal Latinos have settled in hopes of working and creating a better life for their families back home. In these neighborhoods, young women who were illegally brought into the country with promises of jobs and fortune are forced into the sex trade.

Along some of these same forementioned neighborhoods, also thrives a growing Asian community and with it is the same element of human trafficking. Young Asian women lured here with the promise of work and shelter end up in the numerous massage parlors around town offering sex under the guise of therapy.

The philosophy behind music video and pop culture has become many's reality. Instead of art imitating life, life now imitates art. And when I say art, I use that term very loosely. I've learned a very common term that seems to echo time and time again in Atlanta—"You have to fake it before you make it." I suspect that many get trapped somewhere between that line of reality and fallacy.

I've met hundreds of girls who entered into the escort service. They all had one thing in common. They all felt that they were doing what "they had to do." Could you imagine giving your body to a total stranger because you felt that your back was up against the wall and you did not have an out? Any stranger could walk through that door as long as he had that required fee.

To: Dakota, Aliza, Caramel, Princess, Chastity, Shi, Brown Sugar, Diamond and the numerous other colorful names that these girls go by. I wish you the best and hope and pray that you've found a better way. Sex sells but what are you really compromising in exchange? No judgment, just an honest question.

# ABOUT THE AUTHOR

Ceasar Mason is a first generation Trinidadian-American. He was born in Brooklyn, New York, to parents that migrated to the United States in the late sixties. His formidable years were spent on the southern Caribbean island of Trinidad. Between the ages of four and ten, he was immersed in the culture and rich heritage that Trinidad had to offer. It was during this period that he developed a strong discipline and work ethic, to which he credits his Aunt Monica (God bless her soul) who raised him during this time.

He returned to Crown Heights, Brooklyn in the early eighties as the crack epidemic began. Ceasar attended P.S. 221 and Mahalia Jackson I.S. 391, later graduating from George Westinghouse High School in downtown Brooklyn. Like many young men of his day, the allure of the streets was more fascinating than higher learning. After an arrest that landed him in Baltimore, Maryland's Herman L. Toulson boot camp, he realized that he had a talent to write. Writing letters to the courts on behalf of other inmates became the norm as well as writing personal letters to smooth over girlfriends on the outside.

Upon graduation from boot camp, Ceasar remained in Baltimore where he enrolled at Morgan State University's business management program. He would never return to the streets. In 1997 he moved to Atlanta, Georgia where he currently strives as an entrepreneur. He visits his native New York often but certainly prefers the winters of the South.

# RESOURCES

According to "A Future Not a Past", there are as many as 300,000 American children at risk for being commercially sexually exploited each year in our neighborhoods, through escort services and online.

The Polaris Project sites that while statistics on the scope of sex trafficking in escort services are not available, a 2008 study provides insight into the dynamics of the network. Of the women and girls interviewed, 41 percent of the women and girls were escorts, and 28 percent started as escorts when first recruited into commercial sex. Ninety-three percent had pimps when they were first recruited. Of the 41 percent who were escorts, 67 percent had experienced violence by their pimps and 59 percent said that they had been coerced. *(Source: Jody Raphael and Jessica Ashley. Domestic Sex Trafficking of Chicago Women and Girls. Illinois Criminal Justice Information Authority and DePaul University College of Law, 2008. 8, 10, 25.)*

For more information on how you can help victims of Human Trafficking or if you are a victim and want help, please contact one of the organizations listed below:

**A Future Not a Past (National)**
415.441.0706
www.afnap.org

**A Future Not a Past (Juvenile Justice Fund, Georgia)**
404.612.4628
www.afuturenotapast.org

**Coalition Against Trafficking in Women**

www.catwinternational.org

**Georgia Care Connection Office (GCCO)**

404.602.0068

www.georgiacareconnection.com

**Polaris Project**

Nation Human Trafficking Resource Center (NHTRC)

1.888.3737.888

www.polarisproject.org

**Tapestri, Inc**

404.299.2185

www.tapestri.org

**U.S. Department of State Office to Combat and Monitor Trafficking in Persons**

www.state.gov/g/tip

---

## References

A Future Not a Past. (n.d). Retrieved August 17, 2011, from http://afnap.org

Polaris Project. (n.d). Retrieved August 1, 2011, from www.polarisproject.org

*The following information is taken from "Results", a 2010 publication by A Future. Not a Past.*

Did you know? Georgia has some of the nation's toughest laws to punish criminals convicted of the prostitution of children and human trafficking. Under Georgia law, those convicted of soliciting sex from or pimping a child younger than 18 can be sentenced to five to 20 years in prison plus asset forfeiture under state pandering statutes – or 10 to 20 years in prison under the state's human-trafficking laws.

More girls in Georgia are affected by prostitution in one MONTH

than are affected by other epidemics in one YEAR.

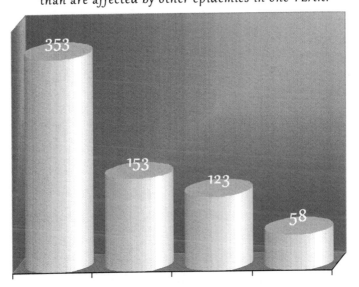

Girls prostituted in one MONTH — 353

Teens known to have AIDS — 153

Teen suicides in one year — 123

Girls killed each year in car accidents — 58

OnCall

Escorting in Atlanta

*Ceasar Mason*

$13.95
ISBN 978-0-9838166-0-7
51395>
9 780983 816607

72358522R10132

Made in the USA
Columbia, SC
18 June 2017